2041

Other books by Jane Yolen:

The Pit Dragon Trilogy:
Dragon's Blood
Heart's Blood
A Sending of Dragons

2041

TWELVE SHORT STORIES ABOUT THE FUTURE BY TOP SCIENCE FICTION WRITERS

SELECTED AND EDITED BY

JANE YOLEN

With an Introduction by Jane Yolen

Delacorte Press

Published by
Delacorte Press
Bantam Doubleday Dell Publishing Group, Inc.
666 Fifth Avenue
New York, New York 10103

A verson of "Free Day" was first published in *Tales of the Unanticipated, no.* 2 (Spring 1987), published by Rune Press under the auspices of the Minnesota Science Fiction Society, copyright © 1987 by Peg Kerr.

"Much Ado About [Censored]" Copyright © 1987 Davis Publications. Previously published as "Ado," *Isaac Asimov's Science Fiction Magazine*, January 1988.

Both stories have been altered considerably for publication in this book.

Design: Stanley S. Drate/Folio Graphics Co. Inc.

Library of Congress Cataloging in Publication Data

2041 : twelve stories about the future by top science
fiction writers / selected and edited by Jane Yolen.
p. cm.
Summary: Twelve fictional stories about school life, fads, inventions, and cultural activities in the future by such authors as Connie Willis, Peg Kerr, and Bruce Coville.
ISBN 0-385-30445-5
1. Science fiction, American. 2. Children's stories, American.
[1. Science fiction. 2. Short stories.] I. Yolen, Jane.
PZ5.A18 1991
[Fic]—dc20 90-20788 CIP AC

Manufactured in the United States of America

September 1991

10 9 8 7 6 5 4 3 2 1

BVG

For the members of SFWA—
they know who they are!

CONTENTS

Introduction
A DAY IN THE LIFE

Fifty years can bring a lot of changes in a culture. I am fifty years old. When I was a baby, there was no television. When I was a child, the first atom bomb was dropped. When I was a young adult, the computer revolution really began. As an adult I have seen the invention of the video cassette, the CD player, the Walkman, the laptop computer, and throwaway diapers. Rock and roll, electronic music, the Pill, heart and liver transplants, fast food chains, fax machines, polio vaccines, AIDS, the depleted ozone layer were all born after I was born.

So what will it be like fifty years in the future—in 2041? When *you* are in your sixties?

Without a time machine we can't make absolute predictions, of course. But science fiction writers have been in the business of writing stories that project certain fads, certain fancies, certain inventions, certain cultural activities into the future. So these twelve stories are possible glimpses into possible futures.

What will school be like? Patricia McKillip obviously thinks computers will play even more of a role than they do now, while Susan Shwartz looks at schools on space habitats. Connie Willis, on the other hand, looks at what could happen if current trends toward book censoring in our schools continue.

What will teens do for fun? How about rock-and-roll gangs? Nancy Springer suggests that teenage music will *really* be an outlaw activity, while I wonder about rock-and-roll deafness, which is already a problem today. Anne McCaffrey explores the idea that the horse will be an endangered species and protected in a special way, so that horse-crazy kids will really have to go a long way for a ride. Joe Haldeman invents a kind of flying gymnastics. And Resa Nelson and David Alexander Smith look at the future of—of all things—baseball. How about those Red Sox?

Teens will still have jobs—at least Kara Dalkey and Peg Kerr think so, though they have very different ideas about what kind of jobs and what kind of communities those jobs will be in.

And diets? You wouldn't want to try Carol Farley's!

And politics? Bruce Coville's hard-hitting story that ends this book will give you a lot to think about.

Thinking about, of course, is what science fiction stories do best. The authors think a lot about the future—and they make you think as well.

These stories aren't necessarily what *will* happen, though many of them carry warnings in their bones. They are about what *could* happen.

But please notice—all the authors in this book

believe there *will be* a future. 2041 will come and human beings will be around to enjoy it.

Perhaps we can all plan to meet then and compare notes: who was right, who was close, who was way off the mark. After all, Leonardo daVinci devised a parachute on paper hundreds of years before one was actually invented. Jules Verne's Captain Nemo rode around in a submarine before any such ship was on the drawing boards. But for every right guess, there have been thousands of wrong ones. Science fiction writers wrote hundreds of stories about landing on the moon before July 1969, and their characters went on boats, in airplanes, in hot-air balloons, in time machines, and were carried there by moon men. A few even went by rocket.

My own children watched that 1969 moon landing on television. They were very young. They fully expect to be around to see people on Mars. And if scientists keep working on extending our life spans, I may even be around to see it as well. In 2041. When *you* are in your sixties. And I am 102.

—JANE YOLEN

2041

1

MUCH ADO ABOUT [CENSORED]

Connie Willis

"I did it, Becky," Portia shouted at me from the forty-yard line. "I talked her into it!"

Bobby Nonecke was pounding my head into the ground so I couldn't hear who she'd talked into what. Portia can talk just about anybody into anything. I mean, last year she'd talked the cafeteria cooks into actually serving edible food for a couple of weeks. I wondered if I could get her to talk Bobby Nonecke into not beating me to a pulp every day during scrimmage. I doubted it.

"Let me up, you big baboon," I said to Bobby. "I've got to talk to Portia."

He bounced my head off the grass a couple more times and let me up, then ambled off to find some other victim.

Portia ran onto the field. "I talked Harrows into it, Becky," she said.

"Into what?" I said, spitting into my hand to see if any teeth came out.

"Into teaching *The Merchant of Venice,* " she said.

Bobby must have knocked part of my brains loose. Harrows is our English lit teacher, and nobody's ever talked her into anything, certainly not teaching Shakespeare. I took off my helmet and examined it for gray matter.

"I told her she had to teach it," Portia said, "because I was named after the main character, and I'd never even read it."

"And that convinced her?" I said.

"Yes," she said, looking as guilty as Portia ever does, which isn't very. One of the reasons Portia is so successful at talking people into things is that she isn't above using blackmail. That time in the cafeteria she found out what they put in the pizza bytes and threatened to show the recipe on the video announcements if the cooks didn't stop serving things that tasted like toxic waste.

"What did you threaten her with?" I said.

"Nothing! I told her the National Task Force on the Use of the Classics in the Public Schools recommended teaching Shakespeare, and she said okay."

"Just like that?"

"No, of course not 'just like that.' She says we have to help her get it ready."

"I can't," I said. "I've got football practice till six." I put my helmet back on.

"I told her that, and she said we could come in tomorrow morning before class."

"How did I get roped into this?" I said. "I'm not named after a character in *The Merchant of Venice.* "

"But you're my best friend and you want an A in English lit and this is your chance to read Shakespeare!"

I told you she was good at talking people into things. "What time tomorrow morning?" I said, velcroing my helmet in place.

"Seven!" she said. "Hi, Bobby. See you tomorrow morning, Becky." She waved good-bye and ran off the field.

I turned around. Bobby was standing there. "Coach says she wants us to practice tackles," he said, and dived for my knees. "What'd Portia want?" he asked as my face hit the ground. "Did she talk the principal into calling a snow day again?"

"Oof," I said. "No. We're studying Shakespeare in English lit."

He let go of my knees and stood up. "Don't kid around," he said. "What'd she really want?"

I hobbled into Harrows's room at seven the next morning. Nobody was there. I sat down in one of the desks, trying not to let any of my bruises, scrapes, or wounds touch anything. Bobby Nonecke had practiced tackling me about two thousand times before Coach blew her whistle. I'd hardly been able to crawl out of bed.

After a few minutes Portia came in, carrying a stack of green and lavender printouts almost as tall as she was.

"Where's Harrows?" I asked.

"Down in the library. She's getting the *Collected Works of Shakespeare* out of the vault." She staggered over to Harrows's desk and dumped them on top of it.

"What's that?" I said. "*The Collected Works of Everybody Else*?"

"No," she said. "These are the protests."

Harrows came in carrying a pink and blue stack almost as big as the first one.

"Is that *The Collected Works of Shakespeare*?" I asked.

"No," she said, setting them down carefully on Portia's stack. "They're the rest of the protests." She pulled a minidisk out of her pocket. "Here's *The Collected Works*." She fed it into her desk and pushed the stack of printouts over so she could see the monitor. "The protests are usually on disk too, but the football team is using the rest of the computers." The stack of printouts started to topple, and she made a grab for it. "Look, this is going to be a lot of work. Are you sure you want to do it?"

She was looking at me, not Portia, but Portia immediately said, "Of course we want to do it, don't we, Becky? Just think, *The Merchant of Venice*!"

"Now, I never promised you *The Merchant of Venice*. In fact," Harrows said, unfolding lavender printouts like a giant accordion, "I'm almost sure there's an injunction against it."

"Well, I don't care," Portia said. "I still want to do Shakespeare. What do we do?"

"First, we go through the lawsuits and court orders," she said, handing Portia the green printouts and motioning me to sit down at her desk. "Then, if there are any plays left, we do the line-by-lines. Becky, call up the catalog."

I typed in DIRECTORY on the old-fashioned keyboard. I didn't like the sound of that "if there are any plays left." We'd probably do all this work and then still not get to do Shakespeare, but I felt better when the catalog came up. Shakespeare had written a lot of plays. There couldn't be injunctions against all of them.

"There are witchcraft lawsuits pending against *Macbeth, A Midsummer Night's Dream, The Winter's Tale,* and *Richard III,*" Portia said, unfolding green sheets one after the other.

"*Richard III*?" Harrows said. "There isn't any witchcraft in *Richard III.*"

"Oops, sorry," Portia said. "That one's a slander suit. It was filed by Richard III's great-great-great-"—she stopped and counted—"fourteen greats great-grandson. He says there's no proof his great-great-whatever killed the little princes in the tower. Did he?"

"Of course he killed them," Harrows said, starting on the lavender stack. "*Richard III* is on this list too. The Royal Society for the Restoration of Divine Right of Kings has an injunction against all the history plays."

She read them out, unfolding sheets as she went, and I deleted *Henry IV,* Parts I and II, all the Richards, and the rest of the list. It only left about half the plays.

"What about *Othello*?" I asked.

"Panpobble," I thought Harrows said.

"What?" I said.

"PANPOBIL. People Against Negative Portrayals of Blacks in Literature."

"Oh," I said. The next one on the list was *The Merchant of Venice*.

"I was sure there was an injunction against it," Harrows said, digging around in the heap of printouts.

"There is," Portia said. She was staring at a green printout.

"Who filed it?" I asked, feeling sorry for her. "PANPOJIL?"

"No," she said, sounding disgusted. "The American Bar Association. And Morticians International. They object to the use of the word *casket* in Act III."

The bell for first period rang before we finished the plays. We stuck the pink and blue protests in Harrows's desk drawers and wadded up the rest of them and stuck them in the recycler. Harrows took the Shakespeare disk back down to the vault while the class wandered in. The minute she got back, Bobby Nonecke raised his hand and said, "Is it true you're going to teach Shakespeare?"

"Yes," Harrows said.

Delilah Barbour immediately stood up, grabbed her books, and flounced out.

"I'm going to lecture on Shakespeare's life tomorrow, and the day after we'll begin reading him," Harrows said. She started passing out release/refusal slips. "You need to bring these back by tomorrow. Protests may be filed through the principal's office."

"Are we going to read all his plays?" Wendy asked.

I don't know where Wendy's been all her life. Definitely not in this school, possibly not in this universe.

"We'll see," Harrows said.

Bobby raised his hand again. "Are you going to give equal time to the theory that Shakespeare was really Francis Bacon?" he asked.

The news about us doing Shakespeare was all over the school by lunchtime. "I wish we could do Shakespeare in American lit," one of the seniors said. "All we get to read is *Little Women*."

"Shakespeare's English," I said.

"Well, Dickens then, or one of the other American writers."

We went outside to eat on the steps. "I still don't see how you talked Harrows into this," I said, sticking a straw in my box of Coke. "You didn't blackmail her or anything, did you?"

"Of course not," Portia said. She unrolled one of her meat peels, laid a cheezo skin on it, and rolled them up together. "I just appealed to her love of Shakespeare."

Delilah flounced up the steps wearing a red "Juniors Against Devil Worship in the Schools" V-shirt and short shorts. She was carrying a sign that read "Shakespare Is Satin's Spokesman." *Shakespeare* and *Satan* were both misspelled.

" 'Ye have sinned a great sin,' " Delilah quoted, pointing at us with her sign. " 'Blot me, I pray thee, out of thy book which thou has written.' Exodus, chapter thirty-two, verse thirty."

"Oh, go away," Portia said. "You know you're just doing this so you can ditch class and get a tan."

"Psalms sixty-nine: twenty-eight," Delilah said, waggling the sign in Portia's face. " 'Let them be blotted out of the book.' "

Harrows gave us passes to get out of our afternoon classes and got somebody to take hers so we could finish up the lawsuits.

The Angry Women's Alliance had filed sexism suits against *Taming of the Shrew* and *Much Ado About Nothing*. *Romeo and Juliet* had five different injunctions against it. They claimed it promoted suicide, drug abuse, teen marriages, duels, and lying to your parents.

There were a bunch of plagiarism suits, claiming Shakespeare had stolen the ideas for *Troilus and Cressida* from Chaucer, *The Comedy of Errors* from some Greek guy, and almost everything else from Holinshed's *Chronicles*. By the time I'd deleted all of those, the only two plays left were *As You Like It* and *Hamlet*.

"Good heavens," Harrows said. "How did they miss *Hamlet*?"

"Are you sure about *As You Like It*?" Portia asked, wading through heaps of lavender printout. "I thought somebody'd filed a restraining order against it."

"Probably the Mothers Against Transvestites," Harrows said. "Rosalind dresses up like a man in Act II."

Portia disappeared into the printouts. "No, here it is." She came up holding several meters of green printout. "The Wildlife Club." She looked up. " 'Destructive attitudes toward the environment.' What destructive attitudes? I thought *As You Like It* was set in a forest."

"It is," Harrows said. "Orlando carves Rosalind's name on a tree."

I'd hoped Harrows would give me a pass to get out of football practice so we could work on the line-by-lines, but she said she needed to run to the drugstore for some aspirin peels.

"I know your mother's chairperson of the President's Task Force, Becky," she said, holding her head, "but I do wish you hadn't picked Shakespeare. He always gives me a headache."

"Since when is my mother chairperson of the President's Task Force on Classics in the Schools?" I demanded as soon as we got outside. "What if she checks and finds out it isn't true?"

"She won't," Portia said. "She's too busy doing protests. Come on, I'll walk you out to the football field." She pushed open the front door.

Delilah poked her sign at us. She'd changed out of her V-shirt and into a skimp top with "Shakespeare Was the Antichrist" embroidered on it. " 'Many of them brought their books together and burned them,' " she quoted. "Acts nineteen: nineteen."

" 'Look not upon me because I am black, because the sun hath looked upon me,' " Portia said, and went on down the steps.

"Where did you get that?" I whispered as soon as we were out of Delilah's hearing.

"The Bible," she said. "I borrowed it from her sister Jezebel."

Bobby Nonecke was waiting for us on the sidelines. "Coach says we're supposed to learn some new defense moves."

That was the best news I'd had in a long time. All we had to do was run simulations on a computer. After doing the protests it would be a breeze.

I waved good-bye to Portia and started for the locker room.

"Which of Bacon's plays is Harrows doing?" Bobby said.

"*Hamlet*," I said, and my chin hit the ground. The rest of me hit even harder. "What the heck was that?" I asked, trying to get up.

"A new defense," he said, and showed it to me again.

It took a real effort to drag my bruised and battered body into school the next morning. Portia was already there.

"Are you going to start Shakespeare today?" she asked Harrows.

"If everybody remembers to bring in their release/refusal slips and if there aren't any more of these." She handed Portia a yellow printout.

"What is it?" I asked.

"Delilah," Portia said. She read out loud from the paper. " 'Ms. Harrows is preaching promiscuity, birth control, and abortion by saying Shakespeare got Anne Hathaway pregnant before they got married.' "

"You will notice that *promiscuity, abortion, pregnant,* and *before* are all misspelled," Harrows said. "Actually, there are fewer misspellings than in the one her sister Jezebel filed last year. Jezebel accused me of preaching burglary, lawbreaking, and gun control by saying that Shakespeare was arrested for poaching a deer."

"And she misspelled *poaching*?" Portia asked.

"She misspelled *deer*." Harrows stuck a straw in a box of Alka-Seltzer. "I suppose we'd better get started."

"I get to run the excise-and-reformat program," Portia said, plunking herself down at the computer and handing me a stack of pink printouts.

"How do you want to do this?" Harrows asked. "By group or by line?"

"By line," Portia said. She punched in the first scene. "Act One, Scene One, Bernardo: Who's there?"

"It's protested," I said.

"What could anybody possibly protest about 'Who's there?'?"

"The National Coalition Against Contractions protested it," I said. " 'The use of contractions is directly responsible for the increase in crime rates. There were fewer cases of murder, armed robbery, and assault in the Middle Ages, when contractions hadn't been invented.' "

"I think we'd better do it by group," Harrows said. "The Commission on Poison Prevention feels the 'graphic depiction of poisoning in the murder of Hamlet's father may lead to copycat crimes.' They cite a case in New Jersey where a sixteen-year-old poured Drano in his father's ear after reading the play." She unscrolled some more pink printout. "The Copenhagen Chamber of Commerce objects to the line 'Something is rotten in the state of Denmark.' Students Against Suicide, the International Federation of Florists, and the Red Cross all object to Ophelia's drowning."

"The International Federation of Florists?" I asked.

"She fell in picking flowers," Harrows said, slurping on her straw. It sounded like the box was almost empty. "I think I'll run down to the drugstore before school starts and get some more Alka-Seltzer. Can you two do all right without me?"

"Sure," Portia said. "Becky, read me the next one."

Harrows went out, still slurping on her Alka-Seltzer.

"The National Cutlery Council objects to the depiction of swords as deadly weapons," I said. " 'Swords don't kill people. People kill people.' The Ladies' Liberation Front objects to—"

"Don't go so fast," Portia said, squinting at the screen. Every few seconds she tapped a key and kept on squinting.

"You're reading the play, aren't you?" I said.

"Of course," she said, not even bothering to look guilty.

"You're not supposed to read the parts people object to," I said. "That's what the excise-and-reformat programs are for."

"I have to read the play to find out what I'm

excising," she said, still squinting at the screen. "You know, I'll bet this is even better than *The Merchant of Venice*. See, this guy Hamlet's come home from college because his dad died, and everybody says it was a natural death, but this ghost tells him he was murdered—"

"Ghost?" I said. "I'll bet Delilah gets that taken out."

"Of course she will. Which is why I've got to read it now. Okay, give me the next protest."

"The Ladies' Liberation Front objects to the phrases 'Frailty, thy name is woman' and 'Oh, most pernicious woman,' the 'What a piece of work is man' speech, and the queen."

"The whole queen?"

I scrolled through the printout again. "Yes, all lines, references, and allusions."

Harrows came back in carrying a big plastic sack. "How's it going?" she asked.

"We lost the queen," Portia said. "What's the next one, Becky?"

"I nearly tripped over Delilah on the front steps," Harrows said, setting out boxes of antacid and pain reliever peels. "She's using an aluminum sun reflector."

"Ass," I said.

"What?" Harrows said.

"Ass," I said. "A.S.S. The Association of Summer Sunbathers. They object to the line 'I am too much in the sun.' "

We were only half finished when the bell rang. The Nun's Network objected to the line "Get thee to a nunnery," Fat and Proud of It wanted the passage beginning "Oh, that this too, too solid flesh should melt" removed, and we didn't even get to Delilah's list, which was eight pages long.

Harrows had me take the Shakespeare disk back to the library while she and Portia cleaned up. On the way I ran into Wendy. "What play are we going to do?" she asked me.

"*Hamlet*," I said.

"*Hamlet*?" she said. "Is that the one about the guy whose uncle murders the king and then the queen marries the uncle?"

"Not anymore," I said.

Harrows had the release/refusal slips all collected and the refusals sent to the library by the time I got back.

"William Shakespeare was born," she said as I slipped into my seat, "on April 23, 1564, in Stratford-on-Avon."

"*If* he was Shakespeare," Bobby said. "Bacon was born on January 22, 1561."

Harrows told us to come in to her room at lunch, but when we got there she said she needed to lie down for a while so we went outside.

Delilah was lounging on the top step, reeking of suntan oil and wearing a string suit. There wasn't enough room on the top half for anything to be printed, but across her rear end it said "Hamlet is indecent."

" 'Though I give my body to be burned and have not charity, it profiteth me nothing,' " Portia said. "First Corinthians thirteen: three."

Delilah sat up and took her sunglasses off. "What about that thing you said yesterday, about the sun turning people black? What was that from?"

"The Bible," Portia said. "Song of Solomon. Chapter one, verse six."

"Oh," Delilah said, relieved. "That's not in the Bible anymore. We threw that out."

Harrows was still lying down when we came in from lunch. She wrote us a note so we could get the Shakespeare disk out of the vault, and we started in on Delilah's list.

She objected to forty-three references to spirits, ghosts, and related matters, twenty-one pornographic words (*pornographic* was misspelled), and seventy-eight others that she thought might be, such as *pajock* and *cockles*.

The Society for the Advancement of Philosophy didn't like the line "There are more things in heaven and earth, Horatio, than are dreamt of in your philosophy," and the Actor's Guild didn't like Hamlet's hiring nonunion employees.

We were knee-deep in printouts by the time Harrows got up. "We're doing great," I said. "There's just one more protest. It's from the Drapery Defense League. They object to Polonius being stabbed while he's hiding behind a curtain. They say, 'This scene implies that the curtain is dangerous. Draperies don't kill people. People kill people.' "

Harrows punched a hole in a box of antacid with her thumb and drank it without a straw.

—▪—

Portia and I ran the excise-and-reformat programs and then I went to football practice.

"We're supposed to practice takedowns," Bobby said.

Takedowns. My favorite thing next to being blown up by a micronuke. "Great," I said, and put my helmet on, watching Bobby the whole time since he usually butts his head into my stomach before I even get the chin strap fastened.

"There's absolute proof that Bacon wrote *Hamlet,*" he said. "It's right there in the play."

"It is?" I said, waiting for him to dive suddenly at me.

"Right there in the first scene. There's a ghost, right? That means the play was *ghostwritten.* Ghost writer, get it? Huh, get it?"

Well, he was just standing there, like Polonius behind the curtain. It was too good a chance to pass up. "I got it," I said, and rammed my head into his solar plexus.

—▪—

Portia and I went in early to help Harrows print out thirty copies of *Hamlet* and then passed them out to the class for her. She assigned Wendy and Bobby to read the parts of Hamlet and Horatio.

" 'The air bites shrewdly; it is very cold,' " Wendy read.

"Where are we?" Bobby said.

I pointed out the place to him.

"Thanks," he said, being careful to keep away from me. " 'It is a nipping and an eager air.' "

" 'What hour now?' " Wendy read.

" 'I think it lacks of twelve.' "

Wendy turned her paper over and looked at the back. "That's it?" she said. "That's all there is to *Hamlet*? I thought his uncle killed his father and then the ghost told him his mother was in on it and he said 'To be or not to be' and Ophelia killed herself and stuff." She turned the paper back over. "This can't be the whole play."

"It better not be the whole play," Delilah said. She came in carrying her picket sign. She was wearing a shirt over her string suit, but the parts of her I could see looked pretty sunburned. "There'd better not be any *pajocks* in it. Or *cockles*."

"Did you need some Solarcaine, Delilah?" Harrows asked her.

"I *need* a Magic Marker," she said, and flounced out, sort of. It looked like it hurt to flounce.

"You can't just take parts of the play out because somebody doesn't like them," Wendy said. "If you do, the play doesn't make any sense. I bet if Shakespeare were here, he wouldn't let you just take things out—"

"Assuming Shakespeare wrote it," Bobby said. "If you take every other letter in line two except the first three and the last six, they spell 'pig,' which is obviously a code word for Bacon."

Harrows let class out early. "Four lines," I told Portia at our locker. "All that work for four lousy lines. And I didn't even get to read the play."

"Oh, yeah, I forgot about that," she said, fishing around in her locker. She handed me a piece of paper about the size of a cheezo skin.

"What's this?" I said. "*King Lear*?"

"It's the note Harrows gave us to get the Shakespeare disk out of the vault."

"Don't you need it," I said, "so you can read *The Merchant of Venice*?"

"I already did," she said.

"We should really give this to Wendy."

"You don't have to," she said, and actually looked guilty.

"What did you do, copy the note?" I demanded.

"Of course not," she said. "I copied *The Complete Works*. Well, you and Bobby were busy practicing defense moves, and nobody was using your computer."

Bobby Nonecke came over to our locker. "Coach said to tell you no practice tonight on account of she's got to get ready to teach evolution."

"Thanks," I said.

"Anytime," he said, holding his stomach.

"I suppose you're the one behind that too?" I said as soon as he was out of earshot.

"Me?" she said innocently. "Why would I do that?

I'm not named after anybody in evolution." She shut her locker. "You know who you're named after? Becky Thatcher in *Huckleberry Finn*."

"Becky Thatcher is in *Tom Sawyer*," I said.

"So I was thinking that next year we could get Madden to teach Mark Twain. It would be better than *Little Women*."

She had a point. We went outside. Delilah was on the top step, on her knees next to her picket sign, crossing out the word *man* in "Spokesman."

"The Feminists for a Fair Language are here," she said disgustedly. "They've got a court order." She wrote *persin* above the crossed-out *man*. "A court order! Can you believe that? I mean, what's happening to our right to freedom of speech?"

"You misspelled 'person,' " I said.

2

WHO'S GONNA ROCK US HOME?

Nancy Springer

"Take the Cope," Jephed's father advised. "It'll help you adjust."

"I don't want to adjust." Jephed Shue held on hard to his guitar.

Their voices rose quickly, as always. There had been a time when his father had been the one to hug him and wipe his nose when he cried and take him to the megamall and show him how to cook supperpak and fix a light panel, but that had been back before he started to think for himself and disagreed with his father so much. His father was stubborn. Never admitted he was wrong about anything.

Their voices heightened and hardened. Mr. Shue flung up his square hands, exclaiming "You kids, you don't know how good a life you got! Legal drugs, free doctors to keep 'em safe, guaranteed income, no wars. . . . You don't know how lucky you are to live in a world where there's not gonna be a nuclear war."

Jephed said, "You call it living?"

"What the hell you want? So it's slow, so nothing much happens, that's what the drugs are for. At least you got security. You know you're not gonna starve or get killed."

Having lived through the turmoil of the millennium, Mr. Shue had given his heart and soul to the new United States of EurAsiaMerica, Inc. There had been terrible, exciting times before Jephed was born. He wished his father would talk about them more often. He wished his father would talk *to* him more often, instead of *at* him. Sitting in the small kitchen, being yelled at by his father, he felt the familiar heartache, yet knew he couldn't give in. His life was at stake.

Maybe his father felt the heartache too. "Look." Mr. Shue lowered his voice with a visible effort tightening his husky, reddened face. "Being a tax clerk third class ain't so bad."

Jephed had finished school to the extent that was considered appropriate for him. His aptitude tests, which pretty much determined his future, said he was best suited for government work. More than half the country worked for the government, though he knew no one who worked for the power behind the government, for the Corporation.

"Better than what I do," Jephed's father went on. He was a blue-collar worker, a robot operator at a freight yard. At some time some agency had decided he was a big, strong man, and he had been assigned to an outdoor job. But he did not like the cold. In the wintertime his hands and face chapped. "You'll work in a nice warm office," he said. "When you get to be my age you'll appreciate that."

"I'll never get to be your age if I have to clerk," said Jephed. "I'll kill myself first."

His father lunged up, overturning his chair. "Don't talk like that!" Mr. Shue bellowed. "Just take the Cope! That's what it's for, to keep you from thinking stuff like that!"

Jephed got up, clutching his guitar, and headed toward the door.

"Get back here. Put down that guitar. Where you think you're going?"

Jephed did not put down the guitar, but turned to face him. "Out of here," he said, meaning *out* of tests and recommendations, *out* of fifty years of clerical work and monitored drug intake and team counseling meetings and retirement planning, *out* of the safe, static, benevolently socialist world into which he had been born. *Out.*

His father knew what he meant. "Look. Jeph. Son." The older man fumbled toward him with a calloused hand. "You ain't thinking of going to the gangs, are you?"

Jephed looked steadily back at him and did not answer. It was no use answering. His father would never understand how the street gangs were where life was, life bone-deep and sky-high, life rich with danger and bloodletting and dying. And they were where the music was too, the real music with muscle and nerve endings in it, not the soft-rock sell-out-to-the-money-machine stuff that the cable radios played.

His father's eyes went hard. He said, "I should

have broken that blasted guitar in half the minute you brought it in the house."

"So break me in half and have it done with," said Jephed. His music was his life. He knew this the way he knew few other things. The way he knew his mother had loved him, giving him life before she died. The way he had once known how his father loved him . . . now he felt not so sure.

"Listen, punk." His father had gone quiet and stony, a stocky rock of a blue-shirt man standing in the shabby room. "You walk out of here now, don't ever come back."

Jephed nodded. "Bye," he whispered. He went out the door.

The guitar's name was Galahad, and it was Jephed's closest friend. For years he had told it all his dreams, singing them to it in the songs he wrote daily. Often he had slept with it, as he slept with it that first night away from home, under a looming, nearly silent highway overpass.

The next morning he started trudging down the potholed streets toward the half-ruined core of the city. Occasional delivery trucks and motor coaches bumbled their slow way past him. There were few private cars. His father remembered the days of fast, dangerous automobiles and crowded highways, but Jephed was not likely ever to own a car of his own. Too expensive, too wasteful. Most people (including government clerks) worked out of home offices, networked to their teams by phone and computer. If he had wanted to, Jephed could have shopped via television, socialized via computer, spent his entire life cocooned in his home.

He did not want to.

Sometime past noon, very hungry, he sat down on a curb by an empty building and, for want of food, he hugged Galahad. He turned on the hidden switch—no plug-in, no trailing cords anymore like in the glory days of rock. Mike, amp, speaker, they were all right there in the guitar's belly. Jephed turned the volume up moderately loud and sang.

"Hey, Springsteen, where you been, man, we miss
you.
Boss got him a bimbo,
Boss got him a bimbo.
Hey, King, where you gone, flushed yourself down
the john.
Who's gonna bring us to Graceland now,
Who's gonna rock us home?"

He let his hunger haunt his voice. Galahad's peg-flanked face was smiling, warmed up to the music, ready for some string-bending. Jephed leaned into a riff. After a while he grew aware of a girl standing behind his right shoulder, listening, and he faltered to a stop, swiveled, and looked up at her. Black leather short skirt, black lace bra top, glossy black hair. Hispano.

She said in Spanish, "You're good."

He nodded. He understood her well enough, for the new America was bilingual. But he did not speak, because she was hard-edged and beautiful and she made him feel shy. Jephed knew he was nothing much to look at. If he had been handsome, he would have applied to the Bureau of Popular Culture to be a rock star and sing all his life. But no use trying, because they wanted people who would holo well, turn-on people who could really smirk and swing their hips. Just as well. They would have wanted him to sing the *bay-bee, bay-bee* music that soothed the public like aural drugs. They would not have let him sing his own music.

He blurted at the Hispano girl, "You got anything to eat?"

She smiled like an alley cat and strolled away, hips swaying, down the cracked sidewalks. Not knowing what else to do, he followed.

She looked back at him once. "You'd be smart to go home," she remarked.

"I don't think so."

"Outlaws aren't real nice to strangers."

"I'll take my chances."

She shrugged, and did not look at him again. To tell him that she did not care about him or need to do what he said, she made a show of aimless wandering. But in fact quite soon her ambling took him into the alley where the Ax Warrior gang crouched along spray-painted walls, waiting. Waiting for something.

Jephed stared into closed brown faces. Afro or Hispano, almost all of them. He felt all too much the Anglo, felt afraid. There was no use being afraid. His pale skin should not matter. His music would make him a brother. All the same, he found he could not speak.

A tall Afro turned his scarred face toward the girl. "Luz." He was the leader; Jephed could tell it by his tough wedge of a face, by the red kerchief on his head, by his curt tone. "What you mean bringing this punk in here?"

"He's good on the ax, Big Man!"

Luz stood hands on her mobile hips, spraddle-legged in the alley as if she owned it, and her tone challenged the leader. But in her flippancy Jephed saw her fear.

Big Man said to Jephed, "Play."

He nodded, but felt himself swaying where he stood, weak enough to fall. He said, "You got something I could eat first?"

"You got half a second to play, punk!"

Galahad was no longer smirking, but still warm and full of heart, still ready.

Jephed played.

He let his fear fill his playing. Galahad sang like a stool pigeon, howled like a kicked dog, wailed like a bag lady in love. Jephed let his hunger yearn in his playing. Galahad wept. And Jephed had gone into a trance of music and hunger, so that the world rushed around him like a carousel but he stood still at its hub, booted and straight-legged and colossal. The guitar gods had taken charge of his fingers; he could play forever.

Luz had gone off somewhere. Then at the rim of the spinning alley he saw her come back, bringing with her others like herself, with knives concealed in their boots, the female Ax Warriors. He saw them start to dance. He saw music coming out from behind the brick walls, drums and guitars coming out to join Galahad. The soft rock that crooned over the digital airwaves was all made of computers and keyboard, all plastic, but he and the Ax Warriors would make real music the old way, with steel strings and sweaty hands and an ache in their guts. No mixer to make them blend; they would have to reach it themselves, that balance, that brotherhood. When they sang, the girls would hear their bodies in their voices. Jephed would teach them his songs, the sad songs with smiling faces.

Jephed sang.

"Old man had big hands,
Old man had strong hands.
Old man stood tall.
Hey, old man, old man, when did you get small?
When did your hands start to come up empty,
Empty as my heart?"

Much later, long after dark, he stood in front of them all while Big Man questioned him.

"You take Cope?"

"No, man."

"Ever?"

"No, man."

"Ever going to?"

"No."

Big Man nodded. "You better not, or I'll come after

you and rip your lungs out. The only drugs an Ax Warrior needs are his music and his brothers and his woman. You got that?"

"Sure," said Jephed. Government drones needed drugs, but not an outlaw. This was no hardship. This was what he had come for, the unsedated life: brief, maybe, and sometimes brutal, but complete. The life of brotherhood and adventure.

Big Man shoved his hatchet face at him. "All right. You hear me." It was an order. "You ain't a Warrior yet. You do everything I say and don't never talk back. You on probation."

Jephed nodded.

"You eat last," Big Man added.

But when the Warriors went at 2:00 A.M. to the backlot biodegrade bin where the Zippy Burger closing shift had just deposited the day's leftovers, Luz slipped him her soggy paper-wrapped packet before Big Man could tell him there was nothing left for him.

Jephed learned fast those next few days. He learned to steal food on the fly from the struggling, overpriced downtown markets. He learned to bait the police. He learned to know the members of the rival gangs—the Freaks, the Rockin' Death—on sight. He learned the hideouts, the empty houses where he could sleep, and the places to stay away from unless he wanted trouble. He learned not to whimper in his sleep even when he dreamed of his home, of his father, and he learned which of his Ax Warrior brothers would mock him—like Big Man—and which would help him through the night.

Ax-Kwame, an Afro, took to sleeping near him and would joggle him gently awake when he started to make embarrassing noises.

"You got to get tough, man," Ax-Kwame would scold, keeping his voice to a husky whisper so that the others in the crowded room would not wake. "How you gonna put Ax in front your name?"

Jephed knew how Ax-Kwame had done it. Ax-Kwame had bled for the brotherhood. Half of Ax-Kwame's left hand, his guitar-fingering hand, was sliced away. He couldn't play anymore. That was what the enemies tried to do: Cut you where it hurt most. Take away your music.

He said to Ax-Kwame under his breath in the night, "I'm not sure I want Ax in front of my name." What had happened to Ax-Kwame frightened him more than anything he had ever faced in his life. He didn't think he'd mind dying, maybe gallantly, maybe saving a comrade. But to live without playing guitar—it was unthinkable.

Ax-Kwame told him, "You ain't got much choice now, man! Sure, you can quit the gang, but we'll beat you blind before we let you go nowhere."

Silence.

Ax-Kwame whispered, "What you miss that old man of yours for, anyway?"

More than once, bitterly, Jephed had complained to Ax-Kwame and the others about his father.

Ax-Kwame said, "Family ain't good for nothing. Not like brothers."

"He was good to me when I was a kid. . . ."

"He don't care nothing about you now."

That was what hurt. If he had said *I'm going* and his father had said *Please stay*, or even *Be careful*, Jephed could have slept silent through the nights. But his father had said *Get out and don't come back*. No love. Not anymore.

He told Ax-Kwame, "I don't miss him. I hate him."

"That good, man. You be brother. You gonna be Ax, you gotta forget family and you gotta get tough. You gotta fight Freaks or Death."

Jephed made himself a knife out of a stolen mower blade. He ground away at it for days while Galahad stood propped in the corner of a filthy room and sulked. Jephed could see Galahad sulking, but too bad. He needed a weapon. Soon it would be time to prove himself in combat.

When the long blade was finished, complete with blood groove, he knew it was the equal of anything his enemies would swing at him. Some of the outlaws longed for the black old days of hand grenades and Uzis, but Jephed felt no such nostalgia. He felt guiltily glad there were no armaments to be had any longer, that all the wars were in the streets while noncombatants kept to their houses in the suburbs, that the worst he needed to face would be knives and clubs and chains. Knives and chains were bad enough.

The blade hung heavy in Jephed's hand. It did not warm to his touch as Galahad would have. He did not give it a name.

Death was nothing to fear, Jephed told himself. In those days when most people lived far too soporifically long, dying early and passionately was nothing to fear. But on the way to battle, with brothers strutting at his side, he knew by the lizards crawling in his gut and backbone that the prelude to dying, the violence, terrified him.

Big Man told him nastily, "We be watching you, punk." But he passed him the fist-grip as he did with the others.

And the Freaks, all boots and muscle and tattoo, oozed out of their alley to meet the Ax Warriors.

It seemed to Jephed that they all came straight at him. And maybe they did. He was the new kid. And he was screaming, but at the same time fighting like a wolf out of hell. He had not known how his own terror would help him and make him ruthless. Because he was scared, because he did not want to die, after all, he had to make the Freaks scared instead, and he was taking blows without feeling them, and cutting at anything in front of him, and he did not know until afterward, when his mind replayed the fight to him, again and again replayed it, how his wildly swinging blade had sometimes found Freak flesh. Or how Ax-Kwame had fought close beside him, keeping Freaks away from his left hand, pulling him back by his collar when the police bleaters sounded and it was time to run. Or how he had taken a cut on his temple that was going to make a wonderfully tough-looking scar across his face. He had bled and shed blood for Ax.

Afterward, a survivor of combat, he felt euphoric. This was allowed, for no Ax were lost, none badly wounded. Victory shouts echoed in the Ax Warrior alley. Jephed crowed like the others, hugged Galahad, sang to Luz.

"If I had a hundred battle scars,
If I had a dream-makin' face,
If I had the body of a holo star,
I'd give you my scarred star body, Babe,
Let you keep it in a secret place.
But all I got, Baby, is an ax to grind,
A dream and a song and an ax to grind.
Old scars, old scars on my mind—"

"You're full of it," Luz told him almost tenderly.

And Ax-Kwame, as high after battle as he, threw back his brown head and yelled at the gang, "Yazoo! We got us a new Ax or what, brothers?"

Big Man said, "The punk ain't Ax yet."

Everyone quieted. Jephed silenced Galahad and looked at Big Man.

Ax-Kwame said, though without challenge in his voice, "I thought Jephed done good."

"He don't fight smart. He don't know the moves. Only reason he looked good is you were baby-sitting him."

"So? He got guts. He'll learn the rest."

Guts? Jephed remembered the terror that had driven him into battle. Was that courage?

"He only looks like he's got guts," Big Man said.

Big Man knew. Of course Big Man knew about him. Jephed accepted this without question. Big Man, the leader, possessed courage untainted by fear, and Jephed wanted to know how he could possess such courage too.

"What do I have to do?" he asked.

Big Man looked straight at him. "You want to be Ax," he said, "you got to be Ax clear through."

"Sure."

"No more daddy's boy. Your daddy told you don't come home again, here's what you do. You go home. You cut your daddy with that knife of yours. You come back and show us his blood on your blade, then maybe you be Ax."

Jephed felt his hands setting Galahad down. They might as well have belonged to someone else. His mouth, too, might as well have been a stranger's, moving while his mind still hung paralyzed with shock and fear. He whispered, "No."

"Not the right answer, punk!"

As if from a watery distance Jephed heard Ax-Kwame groan, heard Luz protesting "Big Man, you're not fair! All I had to do to be Ax was stab a guy. Any guy. Didn't have to be my father."

"You don't tell me what's fair. I don't care what's fair, just what's right for Ax." He had not stopped staring at Jephed, narrow-eyed. "I'm not telling you to kill him, punk. But you want to be Ax, you got to hurt him enough so you can't never go home again."

Jephed felt himself gathered back into his body, and it was scared stinky, and it wanted him to say something that would give it a chance to maybe run away. Say okay, say he was going to knife his father, then walk away from the gang and never come back.

Instead he pulled the long knife from his belt and threw it clattering at Big Man's feet. He said, "No." He said, "I can't do that."

With a lithe, bored movement Luz got to her feet and ambled out of the alley, going off like a cat into the night somewhere.

Ax-Kwame looked up at Jephed with the whites of his eyes showing wild. He said, "Bro, you got to do what Big Man says."

"Sorry, Kwame." Dry-mouthed.

"But you don't understand, man. You don't do what Big Man says, you're not Ax. And if you're not Ax . . ."

Jephed understood well enough. They would have to hurt him. Hurt him enough so that he would never come back. He grew aware that Big Man was teaching him something about courage after all, though not in the way he had intended.

Big Man strode to within two feet of him, looking down at him, a head taller than he was. Big Man said, quietly enough, "You got one more chance, Jephed."

Jephed replied just as quietly, "No way am I going to do anything to my father."

Big Man reached for Galahad. He set a heavy-booted foot on the guitar, wrenched at its neck, and broke it into pieces.

So that was the way they were going to do it. Take away what mattered most to him, what had most nearly made him one of them. His music.

Jephed could have run, he realized later. He could

have dashed away while Galahad shrieked and moaned and died amid breaking strings, and probably no one would have come after him. Perhaps Big Man even meant for him to do that. Big Man took his time destroying the guitar. But Jephed did not run. The amplified sounds of shattering wood and snapping wire held him transfixed in horror and premonition. It might as well have been his own body under the boot.

Also, there was a sense in him that he wanted to face the worst. Courage. . . .

Big Man ordered the Ax Warriors, "Grab him," and those who were nearest to him did. Even Ax-Kwame took hold of him. Not meeting his eyes.

"Hold him down."

They laid him on the asphalt, and now having discovered courage, Jephed found its limits. He began wildly to struggle, to cry out.

"Dammit, hold him still!"

They pinned him to the pavement. Big Man's steel-capped heel stomped down on his left hand. His fingering hand. Smashed it once, lifted to smash again.

Then someone husky and stubborn and strong as a bull barreled in, knocking Big Man flat. And Jephed blinked up at him, thinking: I'm hallucinating. Fainting.

But he couldn't faint, not then, no matter how bad the pain. He staggered up, snatching his knife from the ground with his right hand, his good hand, knowing his father couldn't fight them all alone.

"Didn't want to bring in the police," his father explained to him afterward, during the long walk home. "Didn't want you to end up with a record. So I came looking for you myself. Three days I been asking, and nobody'll talk to me. Then all of a sudden out of nowhere this girl comes up to me and tells me where you are."

"You all right?" Jephed looked over anxiously. His father had taken some hard blows. His eyes were blackening. He walked slowly, and sometimes leaned against his son.

"Sure, I'm fine. Those guys weren't so tough."

Not with Big Man knocked cold. Not with Kwame holding back.

"Lucky for us," Jephed said. "Lucky for me," he added.

"It's your hand I'm worried about," said his father. "They were trying to break it."

"But they didn't," Jephed said. He had been flexing the hand in question. Sore, but everything moved. Nothing broken.

"But they were trying to," his father insisted. He seemed to be having trouble with the idea. The concept of cruelty baffled him. And rightly so, because there was not a cruel bone in his big-chested body.

"Sure," said Jephed patiently, "they were trying to, but they didn't."

"It's gonna be okay, then?"

"It's gonna be okay. I'm gonna play guitar again."

"Good."

Jephed thought perhaps his father had missed the

"guitar" part of what he had said, and tried again. "I'm going to get myself a new guitar. First thing."

"Good," his father said.

"Listen," Jephed said, "are you sure you're all right? Sounds to me like you got hit on the head."

"Sure, I'm sure. I been remembering, that's all." On a steep uphill slope they paused while Jephed's father stood and caught his breath. "I cut my dosage," Mr. Shue said. "One thing the Cope does, it keeps you from looking back much. I stopped the drug, I started remembering."

"Remembering what?"

Mr. Shue walked on again, keeping his eyes on the ground. He said, "Remembering . . . when I was your age, all I wanted was to be a singer."

Astonished, Jephed stammered, "You—you sure?" He could not recall ever hearing his father sing, not even in the shower.

"You keep saying that. Sure, I'm sure."

"But—but what happened?"

Mr. Shue shrugged, toiling onward. "I put it aside, that's all. I put it out of my mind. There were other things I had to do. Stay alive. Try to find doctoring for your mother. And then I had you to take care of."

They crested the hill, walked on awhile in silence. Then Jephed's father said, "I remember now how it was. I wanted to sing songs people would never forget. About toughing things out. Getting knocked down, getting up, and starting over. Survival."

It might not have to be a choice, Jephed began to think, between the Cope and the gangs. There might be another way. There had to be others who had once wanted to sing, then forgotten. He would sing to them. The government would not approve of him. His punishment for not taking its drugs and its job would be poverty. But he would survive. His father would help him. He would build a life for himself, a long life rich with music.

He said, "You think we can do that? Start over?"

"Sure thing, son."

They walked under the highway overpass, left it behind. Almost home.

Jephed said, "Hey, Dad. You remember Bruce Springsteen?"

"The Boss? Sure."

"You remember the King?"

"Hoo! Boy, how old you think I am? Now my daddy, he remembered Elvis."

"He ever take you to Graceland?"

"No." His father glanced over at him with bruised, tender eyes. "You want to go sometime? We could go."

Ahead Jephed saw among many others a certain small, shabby house. And what was Graceland anyway but a rocker's home?

"Nah," he said. "No need."

3

LOSE NOW, PAY LATER

Carol Farley

I think my little brother is crazy. At least I hope he is. Because if his looney idea is right, then all of us are being used like a flock of sheep, and that's a pretty gruesome thought. Humans just can't be that stupid. My brother has a dumb idea, that's all. It's just a dumb idea.

This whole situation started about eight months ago. That's when I first knew anything about it, I mean. My best friend, Trinja, and I were shopping when we noticed a new store where an old insurance office used to be. It was a cubbyhole, really, at the far end of the mall where hardly anybody ever goes. We were there because we'd used that entrance as we came home from school.

"Swoodies!" Trinja said, pointing at the letters written across the display window. "What do you think they are, Deb?"

I stared through the glass. The place had always

looked dim and dingy before, full of desks, half-dead plants, and bored-looking people; but now it was as bright and glaring as a Health Brigade Corp office. There weren't any people inside at all, but there were five or six gold-colored machines lining the walls. Signs were hung everywhere.

SWEETS PLUS GOODIES = SWOODIES, one said. Flavors were posted by each machine; peanut-butter-fudge-crunch . . . butter-rum-pecan . . . chocolate-nut-mint . . . Things like that. The biggest sign of all simply said FREE.

I have to admit that the place gave me the creeps that first time I saw it. I don't know why. It just looked so bare and bright, so empty and clean, without any people or movement. The glare almost hurt my eyes. And I guess I was suspicious about anything that was completely free. Still, though, there was a terrific aroma drifting out of there—sort of a combination of all those flavors that were listed on the signs.

"Let's go in," Trinja said, grabbing my arm. I could see that the smell was getting to her too. She's always on a diet, so she thinks about food a lot.

"But it's so empty in there," I said, drawing away.

"They've just opened, that's all," she told me, yanking my arm again. "Besides, machines and robots run lots of the stores. Let's go inside and see what's in there."

Do you know that wonderful spurt of air that rushes out when you first open an expensive box of candy? The inside of that store smelled just like the inside of one of those boxes. For a few seconds we just stood there sniffing and grinning. My salivary glands started swimming.

Trinja turned toward the nearest machine. "Coconut-almond-marshallow." She was almost drooling. "I've got to try one, Deb." She pressed the button, and a chocolate cone dropped down, like a coffee cup from a kitcho machine. Then a mixture, similar to the look of soft ice cream, filled it. "Want to try it with me?" she asked, reaching for the cone. We both took a taste.

It was absolutely the neatest sensation I've had in my whole life. Swoodies aren't cold like ice cream or warm like cooked pudding, but they're a blending of both in temperature and texture. The flavor melts instantly, and your whole mouth and brain are flooded with tastes and impressions. Like that first swoodie I tried, coconut-almond-marshmallow; suddenly, as my mouth separated the individual tastes, my brain burst into memories associated with each flavor. I felt as if I were lying on a warm beach, all covered with coconut suntan oil—then I heard myself giggling and singing as a group of us roasted marshmallows around a campfire—then I relived the long-ago moments of biting into the special Christmas cookies my grandmother made with almonds when I was little.

"Wow!" Trinja looked at me, and I could see that she had just experienced the same kind of reactions. We scarfed up the rest of that swoodie in just a few more bites, and we moved on to another flavor. With each one it was the same. I felt a combination of marvelous tastes and joyous thoughts. We tried every flavor before we finally staggered out into the mall again.

"I'll have to diet for a whole year now," Trinja said, patting her stomach.

"I feel like a blimp myself," I told her, but neither one of us cared. We both felt terrific. "Go ahead in there," I called to some grade-school kids who were looking at the store. "You'll love those swoodies."

"It's a publicity stunt, we think," Trinja told them. "Everything is free in there."

In no time at all the news about the swoodie shop had spread all over town. But days passed, and still everything was absolutely free. Nobody knew who the new owners were or why they were giving away their product. Nobody cared. The mall directors said a check arrived to pay for the rent, and that was all they were concerned about. The Health Brigade Corp said swoodies were absolutely safe for human consumption.

Swoodies were still being offered free a month later, but the shop owners had still not appeared. By then nobody cared. There were always long lines of people in front of the place, but the swoodies tasted so good nobody minded waiting for them. And the supply was endless. Soon more shops like the first one began opening in other places around the city, with machines running in the same quiet, efficient way. And everything was still absolutely free.

Soon all of us were gaining weight like crazy.

"It's those darn swoodies," Trinja told me as we left the mall after our daily binge. "I can't leave them alone. Each one must have a thousand calories, but I still pig out on them."

I sighed as I walked out into the sunshine. "Me

too. If only there was some easy way to eat all the swoodies we want and still not gain any weight!"

The words were hardly out of my mouth when I noticed a new feature in the mall parking lot. Among all the usual heliobiles there was a tall white plastic box, sort of like those big telephone booths you see in old pictures. A flashing sign near the booth said THE SLIMMER. A short, thin woman was standing beside it. She was deeply tanned and her head was covered with a green turban almost the same color as the jumpsuit she was wearing.

Trinja looked at the sign, then glanced at the woman. "What's that mean?"

"It means that this machine can make you slimmer," the woman answered. She had a deep, strange-sounding voice. "Just step inside and you'll lose unwanted fat."

She seemed so serious and confident that I was startled. In the old days people thought they could lose weight in a hurry, but those of us who live in 2041 aren't that gullible. No pills or packs or wraps or special twenty-four-hour diets can work. There isn't any easy way to get rid of fat, and that's all there is to it. I knew this booth was a scam or a joke of some kind, but the woman acted as if it were a perfectly respectable thing. Her seriousness sort of unnerved me. I looked into the booth half expecting someone to jump out laughing. But it was empty, stark white, and, except for some overhead grill work, it was completely smooth and bare.

"How can a thing like this make you slimmer?" I asked.

The woman shrugged. "A new process. Do you care to try? Twenty-five yen to lose one pound of body fat."

Trinja and I both burst into laughter. "And how long is it before the pound disappears?" she asked.

The woman never even cracked a smile. "Instantly. Body fat is gone instantly." She gestured to a small lever on the side nearest to her. "I regulate the power flow according to your payment."

My mouth dropped open. "But that's impossible! No exercise? No chemicals? No starving on a retreat week?"

"No." The woman folded her arms and leaned against the smooth white sides of her cubicle, as if she didn't much care whether we tried her new process or not. Trinja and I stared at each other. I was wondering if the woman had tried her machine herself—she didn't have an ounce of fat.

"You got any money?" I asked Trinja. As she was shaking her head, I was rummaging through my pack. "I've got a hundred and thirty yen."

"Five pounds then," the woman said, taking my money with one hand and setting her lever with the other. She literally pushed me into the booth and the door slammed behind me.

At first I wanted to scream because I was so scared. The whole thing had happened too fast. I wanted to prove that this woman and her slimmer were a big joke, but suddenly I was trapped in a coffinlike structure as bare and as bright as an old microwave oven. My heart was hammering and the hair on the back of my neck stood up straight. I opened my mouth, but before I could scream there was a loud humming sound and instantly the door flew open again. I saw Trinja's frightened face peering in at me.

"Are you all right, Deb? Are you okay? I guess she decided not to do anything after all. You ought to get your money back."

"Five pounds are gone," the woman said in her strange voice.

Trinja pulled me away. "I'll just bet!" she shouted back at the woman. "Somebody ought to report you and that phony machine! We might even call the Health Brigade Corp!" She leaned closer to me. "Are you really okay, Deb?"

I took a deep breath. "My jeans feel loose."

Frowning, Trinja shook her head. "It's just your imagination, that's all. What a fake! I think that woman was wacko, Debbie, really weird. The only thing slimmer after a treatment like that is your bank account. Nobody but nobody can lose weight that easily. We'll go to my house and you can weigh yourself. You haven't lost an ounce."

But Trinja was wrong. I really *was* five pounds lighter. I know it sounds impossible, but Trinja's cal-show is never wrong. The two of us hopped and howled with joy. Then we ravaged her bedroom trying to find some more money. We ran all the way back to the mall, worrying all the way that the woman and her miracle machine might have disappeared. But the slimmer was still there. Within minutes Trinja had used up her three hundred yen, and she looked terrific.

"I can't believe it! I just can't believe it!" she kept

saying as she notched her belt tighter. "Twelve pounds gone in seconds!"

"For safety's sake I'll have to prick your wrist, my dear," the woman said. "For every ten pounds you lose we give a tiny little mark. Nobody will ever notice it."

"It didn't even hurt," Trinja said as we walked home. And neither of us could see the tiny blue pinprick unless we looked closely. We were both so happy about the weight loss that we almost floated. All our worries and problems about calories and fat and diets were over forever.

In no time at all the slimmers were all over the city, near all the swoodie stores. They've been a real blessing. Everybody says so. Now there's hardly a fat person left on the streets. A few people have so many blue marks on their wrists that you can see them, but most have just four or five pinpricks.

Nobody really understands how these slimmers work. The attendants, all just as strange-sounding as the woman in our mall, get so technical in their explanations that none of us can follow the principles they're talking about, so we don't much worry about it. The process has something to do with invisible waves that can change fat cells into energy, which then radiates away from the body.

"I don't care how the slimmers work," Trinja says happily. "Now I can eat swoodies all day long if I want, and I never gain an ounce. That's all I care about."

Everybody feels that way, I guess. We're too happy to want to upset anything by asking questions. Maybe that's why you don't hear about the swoodies or slimmers on the fax or the bodivision or read about them anywhere. Nobody understands them well enough to sound very intelligent about them. But people all over Earth are beginning to use them. My cousin in Tokyo faxed to say that they have them in her area now and people there are just as happy as we are.

Except for my brother, Trevor. He's not the least bit happy, he says. Of course, few ten-year-olds worry about weight, so he doesn't know the joy of being able to eat everything in sight and still stay thin.

"Suppose the swoodies and the slimmers are run by aliens from outer space," he says. "From lots farther than we've been able to go. Maybe they have big starships posted around Earth, and they're gathering up the energy from human fat that's sent up from the slimmers. Maybe the swoodies are here so people will get fat quicker so that there'll be more to harvest through the slimmer machines. Then they'll take the fat back to their planet and use it as fuel."

"That's the dumbest thing I ever heard of!" Trinja has told him. "Why don't we hear about the spaceships, then? Why doesn't the Health Brigade Corp tell us to stop doing this if it isn't good for us?"

Trevor thinks he has the answers. He says the spaceships are invisible to human detection, and he says the aliens have hypnotized our leaders into being as calm and placid as we all are. The blue marks on our wrists play a big role. He says maybe after each of us has had so many blue marks, we'll be culled from the flock because our fat content won't be as good any more.

He's crazy, isn't he? He must think we all have the brains of sheep. Ten-year-old brothers can be a real pain. He simply doesn't know people yet, that's all. Humans would never sacrifice their freedom and dignity just so they could eat and still be thin. Even aliens ought to know that.

I could quit eating swoodies and using those slimmers any time I want to.

But all those little blue marks Trinja and I have are beginning to look like delicate tattooed bracelets, and we both think they look really neat on our wrists.

4

A QUIET ONE

Anne McCaffrey

"Have you never ridden a live horse?"

"I achieved the maximum level . . ."

"*Have* you ever ridden a live horse?" the Interviewing Representative had repeated.

Remembering her hours on the mechanical surrogate where she'd learned the basic equitational skills, Peri said, "I haven't had the opportunity . . ."

"Yes, quite. Well, I suppose that can't be helped.

"There will be a trial period, you realize?" He kept scrolling through her file on the recessed screen, which she could not see.

"Yes, I do."

"Well, then, that's all now, young Peri. You'll receive notification of the decision in two weeks." The Interviewer stood, gave her one of those formal little rictus smiles that Interviewers seemed to cultivate, and she had left with the sense that she had not quite won the last argument.

But Peri felt that she had won another major battle in her long, private, quiet struggle to have the career of her choice. Modern parents as well as modern educational systems had, as their aim, fitting young people to rewarding, fulfilling careers in the widest variety of professions in a space-traveling society.

Class trips constantly introduced students to possible career opportunities, taking them to aquaculture farms, space stations, laboratories, hydroponic installations. From the day that ten-year-old Peri had visited the Working Farm, her ambition had been to work with horses, whose very existence had recently been under threat. The others on the class trip had fussed and complained about the "smells," the "stinks," the "stenches," but Peri had rapturously inhaled them . . . especially the lovely odor of the horses. She'd always liked watching them move in the training films or the oldie movies. They were so proud, so regal, so wild.

Alone of her class, she had asked to touch a horse, which had responded to her tentative caresses with a soft nicker that had somehow thrilled her. The feel of the warm muscles under the skin, the bright and intelligent eye of the animal on her, its response to her tentative caress when it snuffled in her hand, its velvet nose nuzzling her palm: *That* had been the single most enthralling experience in her life.

Through the ensuing years that sudden fascination did not fade. Indeed, she accessed all the information about the equine species that the data banks in her Linear Residence Complex possessed. She even found ancient books about horses, read all available disks by the currently acknowledged experts, like T. King-Sangster-Mahmood III, and, with avid eyes, watched every tape of equestrian sports available.

When Peri discovered that their Residential exercise facility included simulated horseback riding, she had asked permission from her mother to attend regularly. Peri, in her quiet way, simply hadn't mentioned that she had concentrated on one activity. The *construct* was subtly disappointing—like all things mechanical—although it performed as a living horse would. On it she had learned the basic equitational skills, had gone on to show jump on an advanced model. At least her instructor had recognized her enthusiasm and encouraged her to achieve the maximum skills available on the surrogate. But the simulations were just that, and she was constantly frustrated by the sense that she was ineluctably missing the most important facet.

So, with her goal in mind, she had tailored all her courses, even her special assignments, toward the end of qualifying for the Idaho Preserve. In zoology she had done an extensive survey into the propagation of breed animals. She had studied the stresses now attacking both equines and bovines, and was fully cognizant of the perilous future that needed no probability curve to trace. She had joined the lobby that wished to send specimens of the endangered species out to new worlds where they could flourish and regain the strengths and numbers they had once enjoyed.

When her acceptance to the Idaho Preserve had arrived, complete with hotol travel voucher, Peri was ecstatic. Her mother was horrified that her daughter had applied for a career in such a bizarre occupation.

"What on earth made you choose an-i-mals?" her mother demanded, syllabifying the word to express her disgust.

"You brought me up to think for myself, Mother," Peri said, hoping for a kinder farewell, "and I have done so. If you can be proud of my brother terraforming worlds, please be proud of me for breeding the animals meant to inhabit terraformed places."

"But to do so without discussing it with me at all! And you're leaving today? I suppose I shouldn't be surprised. You've always been a quiet, self-contained child." With that, her mother had left the room, not quite slamming the door.

Peri resumed her task of emptying her cabinets and drawers, realizing that there was very little in them that would be useful in her new life. On the Idaho Preserve, where would she need the gauzes of social life: the platformed heels, the decorative face patches, the baubles and bangles, even the security belt? *That* might deter a grown man, but it would be useless riding a horse!

Her few real treasures of booktapes, holograms of her family, and her comfortable riding gear were all that she packed. Her mother had left a note on the fax—"Do write! Do right!" Her mother had a slogan for everything. But Peri sensed both the outrage and the disappointment in those crisp injunctions.

—▪—

The journey to the Idaho Preserve was not direct since the nearest station was relatively unfrequented, and she had to change twice to feeder lines. She arrived at the Preserve in full dark, annoyed at being deprived of her first view—said to be spectacular—of the natural mountains and valleys. The station was also small, dirty, and unoccupied. No one was there to meet her.

The dispenser refused to supply a beverage and the slots for sandwich or snack bar were empty. Disgusted, she blew away enough dust to settle herself on one of the hard benches—wooden?—and ran through a meditation exercise. It wouldn't do to appear disgruntled in her first contact with her new life.

"Yoo-o!" The loud call roused her from a light doze and Peri shot upright, disoriented. "You the tenderfoot?" The tall man in dusty clothes, hat shading his face in the dimly lit station, hauled a scrap of—could it be real paper?—from under his belt. "Peri Schon-Danver-Keyes? Man, that's a lot of name for a li'l thing like you."

Stiffly Peri rose and, discarding other reactions to his unexpected approach, smiled. "Peri's enough!" She extended her hand and had it engulfed in a worn leather glove and a moment of viselike grip. No one in polite society ever did more than press fingers. Her hand was numb.

"Monty! That all your gear?" He pushed his hat

back and she saw that his face was seamed with lines, tanned a leathery brown, which made his very blue eyes startling. His slight grin somehow told her that she had surprised him.

"Yes." Peri had never been particularly talkative, but her laconic answer surprised even her.

"Wal, how 'bout that!" Unexpectedly he swooped the pak up and started for the door. "C'mon! Time's awasting. Got a long drive." He stopped, one hand on the door. "You *can* ride a horse, can't you?" Peri nodded, not trusting herself to words as the memory of that interview bobbed up. His expression was slightly skeptical and she psyched herself up for that moment of truth. "Last one couldn't!" He sounded both amused and sour. "Great on theory, lousy in practice."

He went on through the door and she followed into a night the like of which she had never seen. She stood for a moment, face turned up to the starry sky, inhaling the crisp chill air, gasping as a breeze actually flowed across her face and body. She coughed.

"Gotta take it easy, city girl." Monty's voice came out of the darkness and suddenly lights came on, showing the aged ground-effects machine. It was something out of a Vehicular Museum—a straight-sided rectangle with funny windows, great wheels all muddy, and flip-up side seats in the back half. There was even a spare wheel on the front of it, a long narrow package tied to its roof rack. And not a horse in sight.

Peri felt an intense deflation. So his question had been idle curiosity.

"C'mon, Peri. I don't have all night. Morning comes early in these parts. And we'll both be rising and shining with the others."

She hiked herself awkwardly into the high seat and pulled the door shut. A slight shower of dust settled to her clothing and she was halfway to brushing it off when she realized he was watching her out of the corner of his eye. She saw the seat harness and managed to secure it without too much fumbling. He already worked the foot pedals and the vehicle jumped forward with a belch and a roar.

Peri scrabbled for something to hang on to as the vehicle jolted them from side to side. Assuming that the ground-effects machine was operating properly, since the driver seemed unconcerned with its antics, she realized that she must relax. When she felt secure enough among handhold, seat belt, and braced feet, she looked out the dusty window, trying to pick out landmarks in the headlights.

Dark shadows loomed and things seem to arch over the roadway—if you could call it that, all ruts and stones and untreated surface. It was quite the eeriest experience Peri had ever had.

Suddenly two huge orange orbs loomed out of the darkness and the vehicle swerved violently away from them.

"Damned critter!" Monty muttered. "We'll have to do some fence riding, that's fer sure!"

"You permit your animals out at night?" Peri was astounded.

"You betcha. Now don't tell me you're one of the

bleeding hearts? Wrap 'em up in cotton wool and doan let 'em so much as sneeze or stale on their own-i-os."

"No, I am not a bleeding heart," Peri said firmly. "Animals thrive in their proper natural environment. It is mankind who has restricted them to artificial habitats, not always suitable for the species."

"Lordee, those are mighty big words for a li'l girl."

"I wish you would stop with such affectations, Monty, or whatever your name really is," Peri said in a caustic tone. "If you are employed by the Idaho Preserve, then you have to have received an education and training that allows you to deal with its complexity and problems. Don't patronize me."

"Just a touch of local color. Most appreciate it." This time his speech was uncolored by drawl and sloppy enunciation. He almost sounded contrite.

She could think of nothing to say so she continued to peer out the window, trying to identify the natural landscape they passed. Monty did something with what she now realized were antiquated gears, and the engine of the vehicle changed pitch to a deeper tone. The vehicle began to climb. The roadway was narrow, dirt and gravel, pitted with ruts and holes that caused the vehicle to bounce and sway. To her right there seemed to be nothing but black space. To her left the slope of a mountain.

"Rather a spectacular view by day," Monty said in an agreeable tone. "Unless you're agoraphobic."

"I'm not."

Peri wondered if the journey would ever end, for having gone up the side of the mountain, they came down on the other, around a second and third. She was also incredibly relieved that she had not been required to make such a long trip her first time on a real horse.

"Is there a reason the station is so far from your headquarters?" Peri asked.

"It's not if we have the heli in service, but one of the vanes has crazed. I picked up the replacement from the cargo bay." He pumped a thumb toward the roof. "The primitive contributes to the sophisticated from time to time." He grinned at her and pointed to a bright tangle of lights some distance ahead of them. "We're nearly there."

As they neared their destination, the orange of the main illumination surrounding the crippled heli also lit up some of the other buildings in the complex. Several were familiar to her from her reading—large barns, feedstores, the stark rails and posts of pastures, and long low buildings, some showing lighted windows.

"I'll drop you off first," Monty said as if conferring a favor.

Peri did not take offense. If the Preserve had only the one airborne vehicle, naturally its repair would take priority over a lowly recruit.

But she was pleasantly surprised when the vehicle stopped at the door of what was obviously a row of individual accommodations.

"We may work rough and hard, but you got your own pad and the chow's top quality," Monty said. "Get your sleep. You'll rise and shine with the rest of us in the morning."

Peri unbuckled the safety harness and got out

stiffly, grabbing her pak. Reaching across her vacated seat, Monty hauled the door shut, leaving her standing in the roadway, coughing in the dust the tires churned up. She walked up the three steps onto the long covered porch and felt around for the door's thumb plate. She couldn't find one in the dark and was beginning to be irritated when she noticed a knob on the left-hand side of the door. With nothing to lose, she turned it and the door swung in.

To her surprise, lights came up immediately. Compared to her family's quarters in Jerhattan, this was palatial. Two *big* rooms, three by four meters each, separated by a small food dispensary and a sanitary unit. The first room was clearly a living space, complete with a communications center in one wall, and the second was for sleeping with all its amenities clearly displayed. No wall units here. The bed looked terribly inviting. Peri made short work of her necessary ablutions, removed her footgear, pulled up the covering, and laid herself down with a grateful sigh on the bed.

In what seemed the shortest possible space of time, a claxon startled her into full wakefulness.

"Wakey-wakey-wakey! All hands ready at oh-six-thirty at the barn." The voice was inescapable and shock had Peri stumbling out of the bed, pawing through her pak to find work clothing.

An odd noise and appetizing odor made her inspect the food dispenser to discover a mug of dark-brown liquid. The liquid was scaldingly hot and rather bitter, but she recognized and welcomed the caffeine jolt it contained.

As she stepped out of her quarters, she was even more surprised to see only the faintest tinge of light in the eastern sky. Lights were on all over the complex, figures purposefully heading toward the biggest barn. The air chilled her through the light fabric of her shirt. Why had she not realized this place would not be element-protected? Shivering, she took time to retrieve the only outer garment she possessed and then ran, for the warmth, slightly out of breath as she joined the others.

"Okay, folks," said a big man, jumping to a crate, holding up his hands. "Monty says there's fencin' down on the station road and there's buffaloes loose. Josh, take a team an' check it out. Main job today is rounding up beef stock for the Centauri shipment. We'll work the north two hundred. Before the heli vane cracked, Barty spotted most of what we need in Crooked Canyon." A groan rippled through the twenty or so facing him. "Tam, Peri arrived last night so she's yours. You others can meet the pretty li'l gal later. Right now, roll 'em."

To Peri's shock, no one went into the barn for a horse. They moved to the right as lights came up over extensive parking racks for two- and three-wheeled vehicles, some with sidecars already loaded with fencing and other equipment. Helmets and goggles were donned and the vehicles revved up, spoiling the air with exhaust fumes as the bikes—yes, the archaic name popped into Peri's mind—crisscrossed each other's paths with seeming disregard for safety before they split into two groups: one going down the right-hand road and the other straight across the grassy land that headed north.

"I'm Tambor," a voice said beside her, and a hand, gloved as they all seemed to be on this Preserve, was jutted at her.

She took the hand, steeling herself for another viselike grip, and gave as good as she received. Tambor was a wizened man, his face grooved with lines so that his age could not be determined. He wore the same worn workgarb as the others, the broad-brimmed hat, and the gloves.

"You look a strong young 'un," he said, appraising her with shrewd if bloodshot eyes. "Let's see if you're worth your salt."

Did everyone use ungrammatic speech, well sprinkled with archaic idioms? Considering the strong scientific background required by the Preserve, she had not expected the vernacular to be so conspicuous.

"You're lucky," he added, gesturing for her to accompany him to the barn. "We've only one more passel of mares to ship out. Just got this one lot left to be conditioned for their ride to Centauri. Cattle are put in coldsleep, but the hosses ride first class. With a li'l help from us."

They entered the barn now by the inset door. Simultaneously lights came up along the aisle and the odor, long remembered, of horse and manure assailed Peri's olfactory senses. Then she stared, for her recollection of stabling facilities from textbooks did not match with those she now beheld.

There were fifteen very narrow straight stalls on

either side of the main aisle, which was not more than a meter wide. She had assumed that the Preserve would follow the traditional ways of stable management: big loose boxes filled with straw, high ceilings, and wide corridors. In confusion, she turned to Tambor, who had been waiting for some reaction from her.

"This is a conditioning barn, gal," he said. "So we gotta get these critters used to the shipboard facilities, hygienic and exercise. This is where they larn how. C'mon."

He beckoned for her to follow him up a narrow steel ladder to an open control facility. There was one chair at the console and a stool, which he motioned for her to pull up beside him. Below, the horses were nickering.

"They know what's up. Okay down there, gals? Time for your dance step."

He initiated a program and as Peri watched, astounded, jets of water sprayed over the rubber matting under the animals. Then from the front of each stall a bar began a slow passage to the aisle, pausing briefly as it touched the front hooves, which the horses dutifully lifted—just like a dance step, in fact. The bars continued sweeping toward the aisle where flaps suddenly opened to receive both droppings and soiled water. The bars retracted, the horses politely lifting their feet over it. The flaps closed and Peri could hear the faint rumbling of conveyor belts.

"On the ship the muck is processed, moisture recycled and the roughage compressed into cubes about so big"—he encompassed the appropriate space between thumb and forefinger—"and stored to introduce Terran bacteria into the new soil. We just compress it and use it as fertilizer in the spring. Now," he went on as the nickering below became insistent, "they get their reward."

His gnarled fingers ran over the keys and initiated another rumbling, this time over the horses' heads. They looked up expectantly. Feed cascaded into mangers and the horses began eating with stampings of pleasure and much shifting of their haunches.

"Now we gotta do the same in the sheep and goat house. Then, by the time we're finished, it'll be time for a snack fer us. After that, we exercise 'em."

"We do?" Peri caught her breath at the prospect of riding a real live horse. She also began to psych herself up again, to prove that her surrogate training would suffice.

However, after nearly gagging on the concentrated stench of goat and sheep in their conditioning barn, Tambor marched her back to the horse barn and up the steps, where he dialed for the snack of more hot coffee and hot muffins, which must have been freshly baked. No programmed breadstuff matched this light texture or enticing odor.

"Now we exercise our beauties. Where d'you think you're going, li'l gal?" Tambor demanded when she jumped to her feet. "We exercise them"—and his gloved forefinger emphatically indicated the mares below them—"just where they stand. Watch!" He tapped out a sequence, folded his arms across his chest, and followed his own advice.

To her amazement, each of the horses was beginning to move, first at a walk, then gradually into trot, and finally, into the canter gait . . . all in place on the rubber floor mats, which were also treadmills.

Peri sat down, totally deflated. How naive of her to assume that horses would be exercised by humans. If fencing was done from bikes, and stock was rounded up by heli, why did anyone need to ride the poor beasts just to conform to historical precedents!

"Now, doan look so glum, li'l gal," Tambor said, reaching across to pat her hand. "This is special conditioning for this extra-special shipment. The mares gotta get used to this sort of carry-on until they finally get to the meadows of Centauri. We want them, and the foals they carry, to come through the long journey fit as a fiddle and rarin' to go. This lot is about ready to graduate. They done real good. They won't suffer from a long period of inactivity. They won't spook from the sounds of a spaceship or go bananas. If you'll notice, the halters give accurate readings of their vital signs." He pointed to the display on the monitor, which she'd been too stunned to notice. "Now they got twenty minutes on the treadmill. *Then*"—and he presented this option as a reward to her—"we go down and give each mare a lot of TLC."

"TLC?"

"Tender loving care: a lot of stroking, petting, making much of 'em, and just generally making them feel pretty good. Horses like human contact. The grooms going along will do that, two-three times a day to keep 'em jollied along. Machines don't do all the work that's necessary to keep a horse happy. Not by a long shot, they don't."

That part of the morning routine Peri really did

like, once she got over feeling sorry for the horses stuck in such cramped conditions. They had, as Tambor pointed out, enough space to lie down if the urge took them.

"Horses spend a lot of time on their feet. They don't really need to take the weight off 'em, but they'll want a change of position now and again and we've allowed for it. Mind you, we had to reject some of the bigger-boned mares." He chuckled. "Can't have 'em castin' themselves in outer space, now can we? Did yer books tell ya how to groom a hoss?" Tambor abruptly became more rustic. "They did? Well, here's your kit. Give 'em a good grooming. You take one side of the barn, and I'll take the other. Slap 'em on the rump and tell 'em you're coming in. They like to hear voices."

Dutifully Peri slapped a rusty red rump.

"Nah, gal, not like that. These ain't fragile shrinking violets. They's hosses, with thick hides that won't feel no fly tap!" He demonstrated with a hearty whack and the brown mare moved to one side.

Peri slapped with more vigor and now the chestnut took notice of her. But knowing *how* to groom a horse properly did not explain how tiring the process was. By the second side of the chestnut, Peri was panting with her exertions. By the fourth mare, she was dripping with sweat and her shoulders, back, and ribs ached. Her strokes got slower and slower until she saw that she was three horses behind Tambor.

"I'll just lend you a hand this morning, being as how you're new at all this," he said, moving in beside the gray mare.

She redoubled her efforts and finished two in the same time it took him to do two. But by then she was exhausted.

Just then the noon bell rang and Tambor guided her to the quaintly named messhall. There was a cuttingly cold wind sweeping down from the mountains and she hugged her arms around her.

"Just you, me, and Cookie t'day," Tambor said with obvious satisfaction as they burst into the big room, a huge fireplace throwing out additional warmth. "Admin crew eat up at the main house noontimes, stallion barn crew are busy up there today, and everyone else is out. Cookie knows what *I* like so you're in for a treat, gal."

Cookie was an incredibly thin tall man with a hooked nose (which, Peri thought in surprise, anyone else in this world would have had modified), a wide smile, and a cheerful disposition.

"Stew and dumplings, as ordered, Tam ol' buddy," he said as they entered. "Hi there, Peri, glad to meetcha. Just belly up to the table and pitch in!"

"Apple pie too?" Tambor asked, his expression like an expectant juvenile's.

"You got it." Then Cookie affected a solemn expression. "Poor gal. Havin' to eat what this here human disposal unit wants."

"The aroma is very appetizing," Peri remarked politely, determined not to judge the food by its color and lumpy texture. She could not recall ever having eaten "stew and dumplings" or anything that resembled *this*.

"Hey, gal, yore hands is sure in a state!" Cookie said, grabbing her right hand halfway to her mouth with her first forkful. "Git over there and put 'em into that there box! Why'nt you say somethin' 'bout 'em? Tambor, you ain't takin' good care of the help!"

"Lordee, I plumb forgot she'd need skinning. She didn't say a thing." That last was added in a tone of approval.

Tambor dragged her off the bench and propelled her into the small treatment room off the kitchen facility. He flicked a switch as he entered and then hauled Peri by her shirt sleeve to the familiar sight of an extremities treatment rectangle. He shoved her hands in, glaring at her so fiercely that she grinned, recognizing his look as paternal. She rotated her hands and felt the healing vibrations rejuvenating the abused tissue, smoothing away the blisters raised by the grooming tools.

"Yore hands'll toughen but you better get yoreself some gloves right smart. Come to think of it, gal, you need a few more clothes. You ain't ever lived outside a weather-regulated facility, have you?"

When Peri sat down again to eat, the stew had cooled sufficiently and, even if the textures were unfamiliar to tongue and tooth, she found it delicious. The apple pie—and she had eaten fresh apples as a special treat from time to time—was an experience for her. She expressed her pleasure to Cookie, who beamed with fatuous pride.

Tambor ate two more slices of pie before he left the

table. He gestured for her to follow him to the appropriate slot that would cleanse their dishes. Evidently one did not take a long luncheon respite, but the meal had revived Peri. Tambor then took her to the Commissary outlet, just off the mess hall, where she was outfitted with real leather gloves ("nothin's better than real leather") and fleece-lined waist-length jacket ("we grow our own, y'know"), and a long weatherized coat, with straps to secure her legs ("we get all kinds of weather up here; you'll need this soon enough").

"That about takes care of your first week's wage," Tambor said as they left the Commissary booth. "Lib'ry, rec facilities, lounge are down this hall. You can meander down there later. Now we gotta get those animals tested, hoof, blood, and hide! They're serial tested until the day we lead 'em on board."

While Peri was familiar with the necessary laboratory tests required for any animals to be shipped off planet, she found it odd to be working at this task with Tambor. When he was discussing the procedures and going over the results of blood, skin, saliva, feces, and urine tests with her, he seemed to slip into another personality entirely: methodical, precise, and quite professional. He gave her a satisfied nod when she had finished her lab work.

Then they went back to the conditioning barn for another session of mucking out and TLCing the mares. This time she asked Tambor for their names.

"Doan get too fond of these, gal. We spin 'em out

in job lots. You could break your heart getting fond o' one or another."

"But you said 'tender loving care' . . ."

"Of the objective kind, gal. Be objective with this bunch."

By the end of the day, when the fencing and roundup crews returned, she was so tired, it required an effort to respond to the pleasantries. She counted about forty people seated at the rough tables in the mess hall—all dressed in utilitarian gear, with weathered faces and jaunty, self-confident attitudes. Her immediate neighbors asked her to join them in some of the recreational activities, but she was too tired to accept.

"First day's the roughest," the long-legged brunette, Chelsea, agreed. " 'Specially if you're working with Tam. He's fair but he's tough."

Chelsea was correct on all counts. Tam was tough, he kept moving every minute of the day, and never mind if she had to run to keep up. She would or die trying. Her hands hardened, she grew to enjoy that early-morning grooming, as much for the olfactory gratification that had lured her into this in the first place. The unique fragrance of horse, the tactile sensations of warm flesh under her hands, her growing realization of the individual personalities of the various animals was the reward she had anticipated. And yet . . . she became increasingly dissatisfied. Horses, horses all around, and not a one for *her* to ride.

The hands were sent here and there, on the bikes,

in the big trucks, on horseback to perform the necessary tasks of the Preserve. She began to resent her very basic duties and was mollified only by the fact that Tambor was treated with great respect by everyone, including the administrators. Not even that trio were called by any titles that she ever heard in the relaxed and informal atmosphere that pervaded the Preserve. Even the exercise facilities in her Residential, where everyone worked to achieve the same goal of physical fitness, were not as casual.

By the first week, Peri had had a chance to orient herself, calling up the Preserve "spread" on the computer in her quarters and memorizing the various areas and the twists and turns of the access roads and track. The Preserve extended over an impressive sector of mountain range and valleys, a bastion of the natural, three hundred square kilometers that were not quite squared, having to take into account the vagaries of mountain contours. She noticed where the base camps and forestry stations and the educational farm were located, separate from the headquarters so that ponderous tour-helis did not disrupt the daily routine or disturb the animals in pasture. She was amazed that some ten thousand horses, cows, sheep, goats, and a small herd of buffalo were resident on the Preserve as well as other small animals and fowl whose natural habitat was this mountainous area.

The main base had once been a dude ranch, Tambor told her, where people would vacation in natural beauty and ride out on long treks. Her quarters had originally been one of the guest accommodations. The mess hall was original, and the barn by the corral as well as the paddock complex. The conditioning barns, the stallion quarters, lab, storage and garage facilities, heli hangar, and the other smaller buildings had been added as need arose.

—·—

She had been there two weeks when Monty borrowed her from Tam and started to teach her the fundamentals of bike riding, an experience she found wildly exhilarating and unnerving. Imagine a vehicle that was *not* voice-activated! Why, it could be dangerous with no single command safeguards for speed, direction, and braking.

"Wal, it's true hosses listen to you, and you tell 'em a lot with your tone of voice," Monty agreed, "but all your experience is closer to mechanical things. Learn to ride this bucking bronco first. You can't do *it* much harm."

She fell off the mechanical thing several times, stalling, forgetting to shift gears, forgetting to brake in time, although she caught on to steering easily enough. She scraped her elbows and the calves of her legs but she finally managed to put the bike around the obstacle course behind the garage.

"Not bad," Monty said with faint praise as she stripped off the protective helmet and mopped her sweaty face. "Larn the tracks and roads now from the main map. You gotta be able to get anywhere on the spread in an emergency."

She was borrowed frequently then, generally about the time she should have been having a brief respite from her work with Tambor. One day she took some tools to one base camp; another, additional lab supplies to the men up at Crooked Canyon who were scoping this year's crop of calves. She fell off twice on the rough roads until she got the knack of watching the terrain ahead of her. She boxed herself when she got back and so no one noticed her new bruises or scrapes.

But her greatest desire—to ride a live horse—seemed as distant as ever.

Whenever she could, she would spend a few moments, hanging over the corral rail, watching the mounts used by the teams: Monty's big Appie, with its spectacular blanket of cream and roan splotches; Chelsea's paint; Barty's dun; Pedro's dappled blue roan. It occurred to her that most of the hands had chosen the sport colors. There were three palominos, two pintos, a leopard spot, three grays—flea-specked, dappled, and iron—two more roans, and the very elegant bright sorrel chestnut she'd seen Tambor on from time to time. Was there some kind of competition to choose the unusual from the breeding herd? They were certainly easily identifiable as they grazed. It was then she noticed that they moved among animals with the more traditional colors, bay, chestnut, brown . . . and one so dark it was nearly black. She liked it best—for no reason she could have explained.

"Does anyone ever ride these mares?" she asked Tambor as casually as she could when she had been two weeks at the Preserve. She hoped the little quaver in her voice was not too obvious.

"Yup. We break 'em all in case they'd be needed where they're going. Reckon we say hasta la vista to this lot tomorrow!"

"Tomorrow?" She couldn't suppress her surprised and regretful tone.

"Told ya not to get attached to the critters."

Peri swallowed the lump in her throat, patting the neck of the bay mare she'd been grooming.

"There'll be another set in here soon's they rig the stalls," he added. "Git used to it. This's what we're here to do, and do well." Somehow Tambor implied that she, too, had done well, and that eased the pang. "We'll just give 'em all a bath 's afternoon on account there won't be no water available fer such nonsense on board." Then he snorted. "Not that they'll like it much 'cause we gotta use debuggers and that stuff stinks."

It did. Halfway through washing twenty mares, Peri could no longer bear the stench and put on a filter mask. Tambor didn't say anything but she felt she had lost his good opinion. She couldn't quite rid herself of the odor even after a long shower and much lather.

"Pugh! Stink! Goldurnit, Tambor, you and Peri sit down at the far end" was the order from the other diners.

"If that's the way you feel about it, we'll raise you one," Tambor said and, with a broad wink for Peri to join him, they moved to the bar to eat their dinner.

"We really do stink," Peri said as she settled herself with her back to the dining room. "I washed real good and I can still smell myself."

"Doesn't last long but I gotta admit it is a powerful stench. But then, it's efficient. Most colonies prefer to leave the parasites back here. Ever think of shipping out?"

"You mean, as a groom?" Peri glanced at him but his expression gave no hint of any ulterior motive for the question.

"Nah, as a settler. Purty li'l gal like you'd do well out there."

"If there were horses," she began tentatively.

Tambor grinned at her. "Yore shore gone on horseflesh, ain't you?"

Peri nodded slowly, not able to confide the depth of that fascination to anyone, even to someone like Tambor who had evidently spent his life with the creatures.

The next day, while Peri did feel the wrench of watching animals she had cared for and grown fond of being shipped out, she was also fascinated by the process. The entire unit of stalls, complete with treadmill and cleansing bars (which would be reattached to appropriate outlets in the cargo hold of the spaceship), were slipped out on well-oiled runners into the maw of the transport.

She, Tambor, and the three handlers who would be traveling with the mares to their new world stood on the center aisle, ready to go to any animal that showed distress. But the mechanical noises had been part of the conditioning and the transfer was so smoothly made that none of the horses demonstrated any strong reaction.

"A nice healthy bunch, Tambor," the head groom said, passing over the consignment note for his signature. "You do yourself proud. This your new offsider?" Peri was given a broad grin.

"This is Peri. Good li'l worker."

Peri felt herself blush with pride at Tambor's unexpected praise. She had an errant urge to wave goodbye as the immense cargo-heli lifted. She did watch it until it was out of sight over the foothills, and only then realized that Tambor had too. He gave a sigh but she didn't hear exactly what he muttered under his breath.

"Yore on the main work force tomorrow, Peri. Take the rest of the day off." Tambor strode quickly away, followed by her burble of thanks. His shoulders were slumped and his head down; he kicked a rock out of his way and suddenly Peri realized that Tambor should listen to his own advice.

Behind her was the empty shell of the conditioning barn, all cables and rollers, a strangely gutted organism. With aimless steps she wandered over to the pasture where stock were having a rest day. Her little blackie was racing, head up and tail carried high, with two bays. She'd never seen anyone riding the little black, but maybe it hadn't been broken yet. She'd heard enough now to know that horses were broken and backed at four or five, depending on the need for them. Most of the animals used by the teams were mares expected to breed foals at some time in their lives. Sperm from stallions of all breeds had been preserved against need, and only if a colony required an entire horse was one bred.

Working so closely with the stalled animals had given Peri confidence. Now, prompted by that still-unsatisfied desire to *ride* a horse, she ducked in between the rails and walked down to the nearest group. They lifted their heads, eyeing her. Monty's big Appie softly nickered what she translated as a query.

"No, you're not needed, Splodge," she replied, and moved on a zigzag course toward the black mare who was standing, hip-shot, head to tail with one of the yearlings, each tail whisking flies from the other's head. "Easy there, gal," Peri said as she approached, holding one hand out, palm up.

Sleepily the mare raised one eyelid. Peri moved closer, being careful to move toward her left side, as Tambor had instructed her, keeping away from the yearling and its quick hind feet. The mare was not in a stable, was not haltered to a ring, could move away the moment she suspected danger.

"Hi, there, gal," Peri continued, not realizing that she was falling into the prevalent drawl, "how're ya doin'? You're sure a pretty thing! All shiny black, like satin—dusty satin."

Curious, the mare stretched out her neck, nostrils flaring slightly as she made identification of Peri. Her nose whiskers tickled and Peri took another cautious step forward. The yearling poked its head over the black's back to take notice of the intruder, but it also wasn't startled.

"Hello, there, li'l gal," Peri went on, close enough now to stroke the nose. Another slow step and she was at the mare's side, one hand still under her nose, the other stroking her neck and down her shoulder. The mare whuffled into her hand, then abruptly raised her head and pulled her lips back from her teeth, shaking her muzzle in the air.

"Don't tell me I still stink of disinfectant?"

The mare stamped but drew back when Peri attempted to stroke her again. Suddenly her ears pricked up, her head went erect, and she stared off to the foothills.

Faintly Peri heard the distant sound of an airborne vehicle and judiciously stepped away. While most of the horses on the Preserve were well accustomed to such noises, they could all spook, and she'd be smart to retreat.

By the time Peri reached the corral fence again, the aerial disturbance had passed off to the northwest. She stood for a long while, watching the little mare move, noting her conformation, everything about her. Then she went back to her quarters. Maybe a good long soak would eradicate the last of the medicinal stink. One good thing about the Preserve: There was no water rationing when artesian wells drew upon hidden reserves deep in the mountains.

After some desultory lounging about after her long shower, Peri realized how busy she had been: healthily tired at night in a way that was never possible in the Linear, no matter how hard one exercised or worked. She also didn't like doing nothing. In just three weeks she was attuned to the pulse of the Preserve in a way she had never been to the Residential rhythms. How odd!

She could put this time to better use than napping, so she dressed and went up to the mess hall. Since she hadn't even had time to explore the research library, she went right to its shelves of tapes on the history of the Preserve. She was in one corner when she heard the voices. Then a phrase stood out and, shamelessly, she listened.

"So far so good, but you know the percentage of failure, Steve." Tambor was speaking and not in his drawl.

"Wouldn't much matter if she failed the last test," she heard the other man say in a rueful tone, "she's good enough on the practical. Seems to fit in."

There was a snort. "Who'd know? She doesn't say much—just sits there with those big eyes of hers watching. A real Residential graduate."

"Hmm. What's wrong with being quiet? That's better than those motor mouths you always complain about. All wind and no substance. You said she does whatever she's asked, does it well and no complaints. Not even when the bike pitched her off. Cookie saw her using the box, and from the reading it was a bad fall. Did the mares like her?"

Tambor laughed. "Yes, and she really liked working with them. All but wept to see 'em loaded."

"Isn't that your usual criterion, Tambor King-Sangster-Mahmood?" asked the other man ironically.

"I just wish she was a tad more outgoing. She's too self-contained. The quiet ones can surprise you."

"Are you talking horses or humans, Tam?"

The two men moved off down the corridor and Peri didn't hear Tam's response. She remained stock-still, one hand on the spine of a tape, the hairs risen on the nape of her neck and a sick sort of cold feeling in the pit of her stomach. There wasn't anyone else they could have been talking about but herself. Tambor had been testing her all along and she hadn't realized it?

A second shock jolted through her. Tambor King-Sangster-Mahmood? The tape she had been reaching for—one of the foundation texts. *Adaptation Techniques for Equine Types on Colonial Worlds*—had been compiled and taped by T. King-Sangster-Mahmood. She'd read every tape he'd produced before she got here. Drawl and all, that undistinguished man who had worked her butt off was the *real* boss of Idaho Preserve. She gulped.

"But he did say I was a good little worker." She clutched at that praise as she crept back to her quarters. What was wrong with being quiet? If she had something to say, she said it . . . *except not to ask if you could ride a horse. You were afraid to ask that, weren't you? Maybe if you had . . .*

She couldn't just suddenly talk a blue streak at dinner; that would have been too out of character. Especially in the vicinity of Steve or Tambor. That'd be a real giveaway.

And this final test? What could it be? If she'd been tested all along and hadn't realized it . . . Worry made her more silent than ever. She wished she could ask someone but, as she looked over those in the mess hall, she realized now that she'd had very little contact with anyone but—Tambor.

"That's a deep sigh for a li'l gal," Monty said, slipping into the seat beside her.

She managed a genuine smile, frantically casting about in her mind for something to add, for she couldn't just grin at him like a fool.

"The mares left today. I was sort of sorry to see the last of them."

"Glutton for punishment, huh?" Monty grinned at her. "Conditioning's not *my* favorite chore but we all gotta do it. Didn't I see you out in the pasture?"

"I had a half day," she said, almost apologetically. "Splodge was friendly."

"He likes pretty gals too." Monty had a very winning smile. "Saw you with that black mare. Didja like her?"

"I couldn't get near her," Peri said ruefully. "Do I still smell of debugger?" she asked him.

"Nope! Or I wouldn't be sitting this close to you!" His grin got broader. "Say"—and he cocked his head at her—"wouldja care to have a go at the big board?"

"With you?" She was astonished.

Monty was a formidable gamesplayer, the solo champion of the Preserve. She had watched his lightning reflexes often enough and admired his strategy, but the game board was a popular evening occupation and she hadn't wanted to put herself forward.

Monty grinned, full of devilment. "Wal, I don't rightly think you'd want to go agin me, but I've a bet on with Pedro and Chelsea and you're the only partner they'll allow me."

She exhaled with gusto. "I think they're rigging it."

"Could be. But I've a notion you aren't as slack a player as you make out."

"I'll do my best!"

"S'all anyone can ask of you."

She didn't disappoint him nor did she grin at the chagrin suffered by Pedro and Chelsea.

"We demand a rematch," the two losers chanted.

"Late to start another one." Tambor spoke up, having joined the audience about the board and players. "We've got some ponies to break tomorrow an' you-all's gonna need your wits fer sure."

"An' I sure as shootin' don't want no soreheads breakin' bones on me," Monty added.

"Rematch tomorrow then, Monty!" Pedro eyed him with a stern eye.

"Sure. Right, pardner?" And Monty gave Peri a friendly clout on the shoulder.

"Sure!" she said, not at all certain.

She lay awake far too late, worrying about the final test and her incurable taciturnity, hearing owlhoot until the rhythmic sound finally lulled her to sleep.

—▪—

There was a buzz of excitement the next morning in the mess hall—an excitement to which Peri, despite her fretting, was not immune. Not everyone was to take part in the breaking, so those assigned elsewhere shouted cheerful encouragements and Peri heard wagers laid. There were evidently four in the breaking team, Monty, Pedro, the dark-haired Chelsea, and a lanky girl named Beth.

"You might as well come watch too," Tambor told

Peri, who hadn't been assigned to any duty. "See how it's done."

When she reached the smaller corral, Tambor gestured for her to take a seat on the rail as others were doing, but unlike them, she could think of no banter or jokes to exchange. She noticed her little black satin mare in the pen just beyond the corral with ten or twelve others that were milling about uneasily.

Then Monty entered the pen, gracefully swinging his lariat loop over his head, and the animals began to canter about, whinnying in alarm. She thought he was aiming to catch a sturdy piebald but, instead, at the last moment, the little black mare seemed to run into the noose.

"Change your mind, Monty?" someone yelled in a bantering tone.

"She'll do as well," Tambor called.

The black had other ideas and valiantly tried to run away from this sudden restriction, head down and bucking, but Monty had snubbed the rope on a post. With his quarry captured, the others were let into the next pen.

"It's the old-fashioned way," Tambor said, appearing beside Peri, arms draped over the top rail. "She'll be a range horse. Doesn't have the quality for one of the advanced schooling saddle stock. Nice enough conformation, a shade too short in the back, a trifle more bone, but that's all to the good in these parts."

Fascinated, Peri watched as Monty walked his hands up the rope to the rigidly straining mare. He stroked and talked to her and gradually slack appeared in the rope. The mare was still tense, head held high, nostrils flaring, but Monty persisted, stroking and then slapping her more casually—neck, shoulders, withers, rump—until she stood more easily.

Before either Peri or the mare was aware of what he intended, he had a blindfold on her. Chelsea and Pedro approached with breaking tackle and the little mare, trembling now, was saddled and a hackamore slipped over her head. Chelsea stood at her head, one hand on the blindfold. Pedro hovered on the same side, stroking the mare's shoulder.

"At my word," Monty said, taking up the thick reins and springing lightly to her back, not quite putting his full weight in the saddle. The little mare tensed on her splayed legs. Peri held her breath. Then Monty sat down. "Let 'er rip!"

Blindfold whipped off, Chelsea and Pedro sprang back and the mare sprang up, all four feet off the ground. Head down between her knees, she bucked and twisted, turned and sunfished, trying to remove the weight on her back. Everyone along the corral was yelling, whistling, shouting. Peri wasn't sure whether they were encouraging the mare or Monty, who kept kicking her forward.

He looked far too big to ride that little mare, Peri thought. *It just wasn't fair.*

"Nope, it isn't," Tambor said, and Peri was appalled that she had spoken out loud. "But he's a great hand at riding 'em out. She's spunky but she's smart. See, she's had a chance to figure out that she can't buck him off. Now she'll start running."

"I don't think so." Some perversity made Peri say this just as the mare planted her feet and came to a jarring halt. And refused to move despite Monty's heels and the shouts and yells from the onlookers.

"Hmm. How'd you figure that one out?" Tambor asked.

She grinned at him. "She's smart, too smart to wear herself out running around in circles."

Monty, with Chelsea at the mare's head, dismounted. She snorted, sweat staining her neck and flanks, but her legs remained stiff, propped like an immovable scaffolding.

"G'wan down there, Peri," Tambor said, and before she knew what he was about, he'd shoved her off the rail into the corral. "G'wan! Monty's taken the buck out of her for you. Your turn now."

Pedro was beside Peri, slapping a crash helmet on her head, propelling her inexorably to the mare who was again blindfolded. Monty grabbed her by the leg and hoisted her toward the saddle. Reflex actions found her settling into the deepest part, finding the stirrups, responding to drills learned on inanimate surrogates. But there was a vast difference to the feel of the mare between her legs, the trembling under her buttocks, the acrid aroma of sweaty fear rising up to her nostrils. Mixed with her own.

"When you're ready, Peri. Now's the time to put theory into practice," Monty said, his grin encouraging.

Gulping, Peri managed a short nod of her head and Chelsea whipped off the blindfold. The others stood back.

"Easy, girl. Easy now, girl!" Peri said, her voice trembling as much as the mare.

"G'wan there," roared Pedro, and he must have swatted the mare with the rope end for she barged forward with an incredible surge.

This was totally unlike anything Peri had ever experienced, even when the surrogate had been programmed for random and violent movements. Peri's teeth jarred together and she felt the jolt through her entire body, but those long hours of practice saved her as her thighs tightened and she leaned back, against the forward motion of the bucking mare.

Buck! Buck! Switch! The mare was determined to relieve her back of its burden. *Rear!*

Unexpectedly the black neck came up and cracked Peri painfully across her nose. She grabbed for mane, feeling her leg grip loosen in surprise at the shock. Grimly she clung, one hand on the rein, the other on the mane, struggling to regain her seat, but she was off balance and the mare wasn't underneath her anymore but to one side of her and she was falling. . . .

For a frantic moment Peri was afraid she'd never be able to breathe again. That ground, for all the sand, had been very hard. Much harder than occasional tosses to the matting around the surrogate had ever been. She was aware of the sudden silence from the onlookers, a congregate bated breath, waiting for her reaction to the fall. She elbowed herself to a sitting position, smearing blood and dust across her face as she looked around for her recent mount.

"Grab her, someone! Don't stand there eating flies!" She climbed to her feet, aware that her shoulder ached, her ribs, that her nose was leaking blood. And very much aware that this was her final test. She rubbed her bloody face on her sleeve as she strode purposefully across the little corral to where the mare was backing away from Pedro as fast as she could. Peri intercepted her circuit, jammed her foot in the stirrup, and hauled herself back up into the saddle before the mare or Pedro realized what she had done. Before she herself realized what she had done. But no flesh-and-blood critter was going to get the better of her. Not when she had practiced and practiced and practiced. All that time and effort was not going to be wasted by one lucky buck of a range-bred mustang. Settling herself as deep as she could, Peri grabbed the rein from Pedro's hand and dug both heels in the mare's heaving flanks.

"C'mon, you mangy wall-eyed bangtail, show me your worst!"

"Kick her, Peri! Ride her, cowgirl! Yahooo! Keep her moving! Ride her out! Give her what for!"

Advice came from all sides and Peri, determined not to measure her length in the sand again in front of this audience, kept after the mare until she settled to a weary trot, her sides pumping with exertion, and finally reeled to a halt, head down.

She got a rousing cheer from her audience but, wiping her face in her sleeve, Peri swiveled to face Tambor.

"Well, now, Tambor King-Sangster-Mahmood, it appears to me that it isn't only the hosses you rough-break here. Do I pass muster now?"

There were a few hoots and good-natured hollers at her question. From the corner of her eye, she saw Monty grinning, sheer devilment in his eyes. Pedro had flung his hat to the ground in a sort of triumphant way. Chelsea was slapping her legs at her impudence. Obscurely encouraged by their demonstrations, Peri kept her eyes fixed on Tambor. He glanced around as if taking in the attitudes of the assembled, but Peri knew it was his verdict that mattered, that he'd been her examiner in all the skills she would need here at the Preserve. She couldn't stand it if she were rejected. She'd never felt more alive than at this moment, with a heaving mare between her legs, sweat and blood trickling down her face, the hot sun above and the mountains around. She waited, aware that her breath was no less ragged than the mare's.

"Wal, Tam, do I?" She'd never been so bold before in her life. But this time it mattered too much to remain silently, obediently waiting.

Deliberately he pushed the hat to the back of his head and slowly let a grin break over his weathered face. "I reckon you do at that. For all you're a quiet li'l gal, you're full o'grit. I reckon we just better sign you on permanent."

And Peri let fly with a wild yell that startled even the tired black mare.

"Did I say 'quiet'?" Tam asked. "Now you put that mare up and I doan wanta find a single sweaty hair left on her hide. Didn't I larn you nothing in that barn?"

5

MOBY JAMES

Patricia A. McKillip

Call me Beanhead. My brother did all the time. My brother used to be my friend. Then he grew eight inches taller than me and could pin me to the floor with one knee. He had stuck-up blond hair and eyes like a shark's. We used to share everything. Then he started yelling at me if I even touched his side of the room. He wouldn't lend me his thermo-treads with the silver stripes on them. He wouldn't let me touch his holo-vids or even let me wear his CD-shades, which Dad sent from Earth. I stole them once. I wore them to the Observation Deck, where you can float around under the Dome and watch the stars turn as the station revolves into the shadow of Earth, and then watch the Earth roll slowly into view, brown and blue and frosted with clouds, looking like it's about to fall right on top of you. I slid a CD of Sun Dog's last concert into the earpiece of the shades and lay back on nothing, listening to the music. I thought about how the ocean clung to the

Earth like an orange peel instead of whirling off as the Earth rotated, and how if it did whirl off it might form a giant ring of water floating around a desert planet, and all the underwater mountains would be dry as the moon, and all the fish in the water-ring would leap in and out of space . . .

I must have dozed off then, because when I woke up, instead of seeing Earth I saw my brother's shark eyes inches from mine, and his feet in the silver-striped thermo-treads kicking off from the top of the Dome.

I flailed against him as he grabbed me on the way. I didn't have any force, and he just ducked as if I were an overgrown baby. His kick took us both to the hatch. The air-lock light was green—nobody was coming in—so he opened it up, still holding me. He pulled us through, caught the hatch grip with his foot and shut it, and the air lock pressurized. When we could stand up straight again, he took off my helmet and held out his hand for the shades.

"Give, Magma-brain."

I looked into his eyes and knew he wasn't human.

For a while, I thought he was a robot-clone, a secret experiment of the space station. They had sent my real brother James back to Earth after cloning his face and making his robot-body tall, muscular, coordinated, and giving him more intelligence than I had ever noticed in my real brother. I poked around the station, searching in rooms marked "Authorized Personnel" and "Closet." I listened to conversations in hallways and in the cafeteria for mysterious references to robots. But all anybody talked about were the elections, and why Grathe would make a better President of Foreign Affairs—which she wasn't running for—than of Domestic Affairs, which she was running for, and how Hormel should trip over his tongue and break his foot so he couldn't run again, since he was the lousiest Commander-in-Chief since McSomebody. All I found in the secret rooms were experimental plant strains exposed to levels of radiation "consistent," my mother told me when I got caught, "with the changing levels of ozone over certain parts of the Earth. So stay out of those rooms, Robert Trask."

It occurred to me then that James might be mutant irradiated plant life.

But he showed no signs of turning green, glowing in the dark, or sitting around in fertilizer. My mother, who was in charge of the plant experiments, didn't seem to know he had changed. She read all his perfect papers, she fed him human instead of plant food, she let him stay up later than me. To me she said: "Are you sure you've done all your homework?" and "Did you eat your lima beans or throw them down the recycler?" and "If you keep collecting dirty laundry under your bed, it's going to mutate into something too horrible for human eyes."

James.

Then, finishing my homework late one night, I pulled the sheet over my head, stuck a reading disk into my viewer, and lit the screen. Usually when I do that, I read one screen and then my face hits the viewer and I'm out for the night. I was never too sure why we had to read old books, but James did it all the time, even while being a mutant pair of dirty sweat socks. So I did it. This book was, it said before I fell asleep: "*Moby Dick or The Whale*. Written by Herman Melville. Retold by Cory Clearwater for Reading Level C. National Heritage Publications." Since I had stayed awake through that, I read a bit more. And then a bit more.

And then more.

And then my brother James breached up out of the depths of his bed, slapped his flukes on the sheets a few times, and blew a fountain into the air. "Listen, Beanhead, it's one in the morning, will you shut off the damn viewer?"

"Don't call me that," I said tersely. He had made me bite my tongue, exploding out of the dark like that.

"Fine, Fungus-face."

"Call me Ishmael."

But he just snorted a few times and sounded, his sheets foaming up again over his head.

I was barely sentient, as my mom said frequently, the next day. I had to ask my teacher-terminal to repeat questions so many times that it went silent and gave me my questions onscreen instead. Beyond my earphones there were drowsy murmurings all over the room from twelve kids at nine different levels: that thought made me even sleepier. All over the big blue ball under the changing ozone, millions of students were yawning at their terminal-stations, answering the same questions for their levels or, like me, weren't. Finally my terminal spoke again, in its other voice, the one that reminded me of my dad's voice when he had talked to me just before he left for Earth, and told me he'd miss me but that I'd be surprised how fast a year would pass.

"Rob."

"Huh?"

"Is something troubling you?"

"Yes."

"Will you tell me what it is?"

"I have reason to believe that my brother James is a great white mutant whale."

From his station where he was listening at random, Mr. Bellamy gave me a fishy stare. I pursued that thought silently; so did the computer. Maybe James wasn't the only whale; maybe all the students had turned into whales through some evil experiment. Instead of sitting still and answering questions, they were rolling freely through the waves, heaving their great bodies toward the sun, then smacking back down, diving deep to where the water was black as space.

"Rob," said the computer's teacher voice.

"What?"

"May I conclude from your statement that you have begun your reading assignment?"

"I'm almost done."

"Very good, Robert! I will proceed to question you on your reading assignment."

"I will proceed to question you," Mr. Bellamy's voice said into my earphones. "Rob, did you really read *Moby Dick*?"

"Yeah," I said, yawning at the empty screen. "Mr. Bellamy, I almost had that whale, and then my brother James made me quit reading. I saw it leap up out of the ocean, with the foam flying all around it. And then James—"

"You can finish it tonight, Rob. I'm pleased you got that far. Did you understand all the words?"

"Pretty much."

"Can you tell me why Captain Ahab chased the whale?"

I nodded at the screen. "It took something away from him."

"What?"

"His leg."

"Anything else?"

"Earth."

"What?"

"The whale took Earth away from him, so he had to live on his ship, he had to chase the whale across the ocean. The whale took his reasons to go back home." I saw the great whale breach again on my flickering screen, fling itself up, up into the light, then out of light into the dark among the stars, with old Ahab sailing behind it, cursing it, while the whale plunged in and out of galaxies, blowing stars out of itself. "The whale took something away from him," I said again. My eyes closed a minute and I saw a whale with James's face, its whale-eyes glaring into mine. "Ahab wanted to go back home to his family, the way things had been before, but he couldn't, he had to keep hating the whale, because they fought and the whale won, the whale was stronger, the whale was faster, the whale was meaner. But Ahab has to win the last fight so he can go back home."

"Do you think he will win it?"

I nodded, opening my eyes again. "Sure."

"Why?"

"He has to."

Mr. Bellamy made a funny noise in my ears; I couldn't tell if he was clearing his throat or laughing. I said, "Did people really eat whales?"

"Back then they did."

"But whales talk to us. They sing."

"People didn't know that two hundred years ago. They didn't have the instruments that we have to hear their voices. You have to be in the whale's world to hear it sing. You still think Ahab should kill the whale?"

"This whale is different."

He made another noise. "Good, Rob. How?"

"It's not just something to eat and get oil from and am—am—"

"Ambergris."

"It's not just a whale."

"What is it?"

But I didn't know. "I have to finish the book," I said. "Then I'll know."

When classes were over, I played free-fall basketball with Cyndy and Hal, which is harder than James thinks it is, since sometimes you have to dive into the basket, almost, to get the ball in. When I got back to our apartment, the place was empty. So I made a sandwich and took it to our bedroom and pulled out the vid-disks James kept hidden under his stretch-shirts. I got my viewer and settled on his bed since I hadn't made mine. I stuck a disk in and turned the viewer on and there was a picture of a naked woman sitting on top of a man with muscles popping out all over the place. The tomatoes slid out of my sandwich. I raised it to take a bite, still staring, and the salami fell out. Then James walked in.

"What are you doing on my bed, Fungoid?"

I jumped. The viewer fell out of my hands. I rolled after it, shedding bread and salami and tomatoes all over James's bed. The viewer had landed naked-side up. James stared at it. I stared at it. A piece of tomato fell off my collar onto Muscleman's face.

What happened next was a little hazy.

When things calmed down, I was lying on my bed facing the wall. I could tell by James's movements that he was picking food up off the floor. Before he had done anything else, he told me if I ever touched anything on his side of the room again, he would stuff me down the waste-recycler and I would spend the rest of my life fertilizing Mom's mutant plants. I guessed that meant my sandwich too, because he was cleaning it up. Not that I would have. He could have groveled at my feet and offered me his CD-shades and I wouldn't have touched a bread crumb.

He said finally, "Ah, come on. Stop crying. I'm sorry."

"I'm not crying," I said coldly. I would never cry again.

"I'm sorry. Hey. Beanhead."

"I don't care," I said to the wall. "I will never forgive you."

"Well, you just—you just drive me crazy, always getting into my things. Last week you got gum all over my best stretch-shirt. If you could just ask first, just ask, just once—"

"I'm not speaking to you."

He stood beside my bed, jiggling it a little with his knees. I could feel his fish-eyes staring down at me. "I said I'm sorry. I shouldn't have done that."

"Get out of my side of the room. You aren't my real brother. You are a mutant walking sperm whale and I will never forgive you."

My real brother would never have spanked me.

I finally got interested in finishing *Moby Dick* when the apartment was dark and James was snoring. I wrapped myself in my sheet, put the reading disk in, and turned the viewer on.

Nothing happened. I realized then, staring at the dark screen, what my mutant brother had spanked me with. I shoved the viewer onto the floor and pulled the sheet over my head. I wasn't about to use James's viewer, even if I could find it in the dark. So I couldn't read Ahab's last fight with the great white whale, I couldn't find out how he killed it, how he finally got to go back home. My mutant brother had broken my viewer, taken *Moby Dick* away from me, along with my real brother. My true brother had shared everything with me, he had told me scary stories in the dark instead of snoring, stories about space stations haunted by ghosts of people who had accidentally drifted into space, who snuck inside through open air-lock hatches and tried to push the living out, and about weird things growing behind locked doors in pharmaceutical labs, and how entire lab crews vanished overnight, leaving nothing behind but chewed-up grav-boots. My mutant stranger brother hadn't been programmed to tell stories at night, or to give me half the ice cream bar he had snuck into bed. Somehow I would capture my false brother, make him show what he really was, make his skin split so the leaves or robot-wires would come through. And then when people saw what he really was, they'd help me find my lost brother again, my true brother James . . .

I was sailing in the dark on a great white ship with sails flung out like cobweb through miles of space to catch the solar winds. Distant suns glowed all around me in the blackness. Galaxies shaped like fishes swam by. I stood on my wooden leg looking through a telescope . . . and in the dark sea I found him, white, glowing, pretending to be a whale-shaped galaxy, but I knew, I knew it was him. And I knew if I waited long enough, if I watched him, he would have to surface, leap to find air and light, scattering stars like water, and then I would catch him, my mutant brother James.

I watched him all morning, how he pulled his socks up over his hairy plant-legs, how he searched his chin for wire-whiskers, how he drank nearly a quart of milk for breakfast, storing it somewhere in his circuitry. I didn't talk to him, I just watched for the mistake he would make to show everyone else what he really was. Once he stopped eating and stared back at me. He didn't say anything, not even "Lost your chips, Micro-brain?" He looked down after a moment, poked at his cereal, then shoved himself away from the table. I got up, too, and followed him to class. Once he glanced back at me. I just watched. Then he went to his terminal where I couldn't see him anymore.

The computer ran through math and science with me before it got around to *Moby Dick*.

"Rob. Did you finish *Moby Dick*?"

"No. My viewer broke."

The computer signaled Mr. Bellamy, as it was programmed to do when we gave it excuses.

"What's the problem, Rob?" Mr. Bellamy asked.

"Nothing. I just couldn't finish *Moby Dick* because my viewer got broken."

"I thought you liked the book."

"I do."

"Then why didn't you make the effort to finish it?"

"I did! I just explained: my viewer got broken."

"You could have borrowed your brother's."

"He's the reason it got broken." Mr. Bellamy was silent. I added, "I do like it. I mean, I know how it's going to end—Ahab kills Moby Dick—but I still want to read it anyway. I just have to get my viewer fixed. I didn't know it was broken until after bedtime."

"Oh." He cleared his throat. "Rob, did it ever occur to you that you might be wrong?"

"About what?"

"*Moby Dick.*"

I shook my head at my shadow on the screen. I couldn't be wrong. Moby Dick was a mutated slime-whale and it was Captain Ahab's destiny to harpoon him right through his warped circuitry. Then I blinked. It did occur to me that Mr. Bellamy had read the whole book. "What do you mean? Ahab doesn't kill Moby Dick? But, Mr. Bellamy, he's a great white monster—"

"That's what Captain Ahab thinks. Anybody else seeing Moby Dick would think it was just a whale."

"But that's just it—Ahab was the only one who knew it wasn't just a whale, he had to kill it because it was something evil, it was— You mean, he doesn't kill it in the end? It gets away?"

"No. He kills it."

"Then what—"

"And it kills him."

When I got home after some free-fall softball, I found James sitting on his bed in his underwear, putting on clean socks.

I stopped in the doorway, watching him. No leaves growing out of his ear, no wires instead of toes. Anyone looking at him would think he was just my brother. I wondered then, if Captain Ahab had known he was going to get killed, if he might have been a little more careful. Maybe he would have decided the ocean was big enough for both of them.

James looked up, saw me standing there. He was still a moment, then he reached for his other sock.

"You still mad at me, Rob?"

He recognized me finally, not Fungoid or Beanhead, but his true brother. I came into the room, not certain then what I had in there with me.

"Maybe," I said. "Maybe not."

I put my stuff on the floor, pulled the covers straight on my bed, and flopped down on it. I looked at James again. He sat watching me with one shoe in his hand, his brows raised. I said, to test him, "Can I borrow your viewer? Mine got broken."

"You reading this time of day?"

"I want to finish *Moby Dick.* I want to see how it really ends."

"Sure," he said, handing it over, and went on dressing, as if he had never been a mutant robot, an evil irradiated skunk cabbage, as if all the time he had always been just another whale.

6

IF I HAD THE WINGS OF AN ANGEL

Joe Haldeman

Marianne Scanlan floated in line, feeling sick and nervous and heavy. This morning the gym scale had weighed her in at thirty-five kilograms, the cut-off point. She'd gotten rid of breakfast and hadn't drunk anything all morning.

Her turn. She floated up to the scale at the wing rack and grabbed both handles. Her palms were sweaty. The scale gave a jerk, measuring her inertia, and the wing man looked at the dial, looked at her, looked back at the dial.

"Thirty-four point nine," he said. He started to say something else and then just pointed to the end of the rack. Number twelve, the biggest set. She'd been using it since the first of the year.

She wasn't going to be dumb about it. At thirteen, she was older than most people were when they hit thirty-five and had their cards taken away. Boys especially would starve and puke and take laxatives to keep from putting on those last few grams. But it was ridiculous. Flying was for kids, and you couldn't stay a kid forever.

She clamped on the ankle vanes and backed into the wing frame. Right wrist and elbow straps, then carefully draw the huge wing over to fasten the left side.

Toes push down, release bar clicks, wings at your side, bend at the knees, lean out and fall. The jump platform slipped away behind her.

It always felt the same, launching. Deep inside you, a sudden wrench that wasn't pleasant—your body noticing that you were about to plummet half a kilometer to certain death—and then the weird sparkle of relief rolling to your toes and fingertips. You'd think a girl born and raised in space would grow out of groundhog reflexes. You're not going to fall anywhere, floating off a platform at the zero-G axis. But it was a long way down nevertheless.

She looked at New New York rolling slowly by beneath her, unimpressed by the majesty of it, knowing that groundhogs paid millions to see just this, but knowing that groundhogs do crazy things. She wasn't going fast enough for the wind to bring tears, but the sight blurred anyhow. She dug the tears away with her shoulders, angry with herself. So maybe it's the last time. Probably it's the last time. Don't be an ass about it.

She checked behind her; the next boy hadn't launched yet. Beat hard once, flutter kick, knees to chest, quarter roll, beat hard twice, three times:

straight down swoop. Wings at her side, the lake in the middle of the park rushing up at her.

People died doing this. Kids who had their wings but weren't good at it yet. You could hit hard enough to break your neck. Or you could drown.

She hit the thermocline over the lake and the wind sighing by turned deliciously cool. Her cheeks dried cold. Two people in a boat looked up at her, their faces tiny ovals. Far enough.

Legs spread wide, both ankles out, right wing suddenly dipped to a precise angle, legs back together as she looped three, four, five tight dizzy loops over the water; then kicked and reversed it, left wing sculling to bring her around in wide slow circles. Sweet glow between her legs. She was going to lose it forever, next week or the next or the next. She let herself cry again and pulled air with both wings, dumping speed, drifting down toward the treetops by the lake's edge, not quite low enough to lose her card—then beat hard, kick hard, climbing with all her might, as the lake rotated away.

Tourists usually found it confusing, even dizzying, to look down from the axis and see all that real estate spinning around. Marianne never thought about it, of course, except for times like now: she idly wondered how fast you'd have to fly to zip through the axis and catch up with the lake as it rolled to the other side. Fast.

Hard to fly and do arithmetic at the same time. She relaxed, ankles together, and glided smoothly. New New York was a hollowed-out asteroid, the hollow being a little more than a kilometer wide and a little less than two kilometers long. It spun around (for gravity) once each thirty seconds. So you'd have to go a kilometer in fifteen seconds. That's four kilometers per minute; 240 per hour. Not likely to happen. The wings were designed to keep you from going too fast; the strongest kids could go from one side to the other in about three minutes.

A beginner was having problems, slowly tumbling end over end, crying. Eight or nine years old. No danger unless she managed to end up in the water. Still, Marianne could remember how scary it was in the beginning. She beat twice and caught up with the kid.

It was simple. She'd accidentally hit the elbow release on her left wing and couldn't fit her arm back into it. Marianne hit both of her releases (the wings would stay with her unless she undid the ankles) and reached out to grab the girl, stop her spinning.

"I didn't *do* nothin'!" The girl sobbed.

"It's all right." Marianne guided the elbow strap back into the release flange. "Just don't twist your elbow *this* way." She demonstrated, rotating her arm as if she were turning a doorknob stiff-armed. "Not until you want to get out of the wings."

The girl looked doubtful, and gave a couple of tentative flaps. "I'm scared."

"Don't worry. I'll stay with you." She pulled a couple of meters away. "You don't have a buddy?"

She started to cloud up. "She *ditched* me."

"It's okay. Try this: wings straight out, legs stiff." The girl copied her. "Now just give little kicks as if you were swimming."

"Don't know *how* to swim."

"Just do it." Marianne dipped and rolled, to watch her from below. The girl gave a couple of stiff, awkward kicks and then smiled as she glided past Marianne.

"See? Nothing to it. Now I'll show you how to dive." For the rest of her hour Marianne showed the little girl her basic moves and made her learn the names for everything. They were almost to the opposite end of the hub when the buzzer on her shoulder gave its ten-minute warning. Marianne "raced" her back, flying slowly upside-down, and let her win.

She helped the little girl get out of her wings and racked them properly. "Thank you very much," the girl said seriously. "Can we do it again next week?"

"I'm afraid . . ." Marianne cleared her throat. "I'm afraid I have to go someplace. You know plenty enough, though. Just find a new buddy."

Marianne got her clarinet out of the locker and wiggled her feet into Velcro slippers. She swam hand over hand to the Sector 4 lift and stuck her feet onto the ceiling, automatically making the mental adjustment that turned it into the floor.

It began to slide "down." Two hours to band practice. Better eat something now. If you play a clarinet too soon after eating, the mouthpiece fills up with spit and it sounds like a baby rhinoceros with a cold.

Better eat something. Or maybe not. The lift thumped to a halt and gravity suddenly returned.

She walked down the corridor to the mall and flipped through her ration book. Maybe just a salad. If she starved for a week she could fly again. Probably.

One of the pieces she'd been practicing for band was a medley of old American spirituals, for an ethnic concert. The words to one of the songs had been nagging her all week, the sad rightness of them: "If I had the wings of an angel, over these prison walls I would fly . . ."

People from Earth think *we* live in a prison, she knew, some of them. Rock walls all around us, a bubble of air surrounded by the vast deadly indifference of space.

What they don't see is that *gravity* is a prison. They live at the bottom of a well. We live inside a rock, but we can fly.

She stopped at the entrance to the mall and studied her ration book.

For five or six years, we can fly.

Cheeseburger. Two cheeseburgers.

7

YOU WANT IT *WHEN?*

Kara Dalkey

It sat in the middle of the mail room floor, its carapace a benign business beige. It hummed malevolently. At least so thought Dorothy, student flunky extraordinaire at Swanson & Higginbottom. She gave the thing a challenging stare. Its single, unblinking "eye" stared back, unimpressed.

Its size and shape were like an old-fashioned streetcorner mailbox, and, theoretically, it had much the same function. It was a top-of-the-line, executive class, technologically edge-cutting matter transmission machine. And in the two weeks in which Dorothy had been trained to make use of this time-and-space-saving wonder, she had come to despise every inch of its silicone, plastic, fusion-powered guts.

"Hey, student workers aren't supposed to do overtime, you know," said Patsy the permanent temp, who was entirely too blond and too cute for her own good.

"Yeah, I know." Dorothy sighed, brushing her dark

hair out of her eyes. "But I've just got too much to do." Dorothy scowled at the long line of objects and documents on her desk, each bearing messages in angry red letters; ASAP, RUSH, URGENT, EXTREMELY URGENT, HAND DELIVER IMMEDIATELY. It was half an hour before closing and most of them had been dropped off in the last five minutes. "Of course they're urgent," Dorothy muttered. "All transmats are urgent. Technology is just progress in encouraging procrastination."

"Insulting our little office buddy again? Hey, transmats are the coming thing, ya know. Pretty soon they'll be standard in cars, just like faxes. If somebody forgets their lunch on the way to work, their spouse can just 'mat it to them. Before long I'll bet you can just call up your local supermarket and they'll transmat a roast right to your microwave."

"Ha. Won't be edible if it gets there." Dorothy gazed out the window. Commuters were already filling the skyways of downtown Minneapolis, heading for home. The Futagomachi Rail Line cars went humming past, running people to suburbs like Duluth, Mankato, or Alexandria. Dorothy wished she was going home now too. If she was, she'd have a chance to try out that DNA-Write program on her CrayPC Jr., or spend an hour at the Misigawa Mall, before starting her homework.

"Say," said Patsy, "have you heard from that college you applied to yet? I remember you were pretty anxious about that. What school was it?"

"Hm?" Dorothy turned her attention back into the dreary office. "Oh. The University of Lloyds in London. Yeah, uh, no, not yet. They're still checking my grades and work records. I've been having such a hard time keeping up here, I'm afraid that'll ruin my chances."

"Too bad you can't stick a note on the records explaining that your boss is a hard-nosed slave-driver."

Dorothy shrugged. "I don't think that would convince them. If I didn't need the credit for my work-study program, not to mention pay my Compucard bills, I'd . . . no, I guess not."

"Get a different job? Why not?"

"Swanson and Higginbottom is the best place for work experience if I want to go to Lloyd's."

Patsy made a face that completely ruined her cutsey-poo look. "You aren't going to major in insurance brokerage, are you? Yuck!"

Dorothy sighed. Time for Standard Lecture No. 2. "I want to get into interplanetary cargo insurance. Now that Mars and the asteroids are opening up to private industry—"

"Yeah, I see. A lot of money in that."

"Free space travel is what I want. Get into cargo inspection, maybe a loss control engineer."

"Kinda the dark underbelly of space travel, isn't it?"

Standard Lecture No. 3. "I'm not a pilot, NASA has a ten-year waiting list, I don't want to go into geology, and tourism to those places is about twenty years away, so . . . "

"So that leaves out flight attendant school, huh?"

Dorothy made a face back at Patsy. "Yuck!"

"I see you've really thought about this. Well, I'd

better get running before Sam tans my hide. Good luck." Patsy zipped out the door with the last of the day's interoffice deliveries.

"Thanks." Dorothy sighed again. She contemplated the transmat machine as if it were a temperamental alligator she was about to wrestle. "And you are all that stands between me and a brilliant career. It is now four oh-five," she intoned at it. "I have to start my homework at six. The more you cooperate, the sooner I'll leave. Deal?" *If you don't,* she thought, *what I will do to you will make the work of Jack the Ripper seem neat and tidy by comparison.*

Dorothy picked up the first item in the lineup. It was a document—a three-page policy digest to be sent to the Drane Udrai Insurance Company, located across town. Heavy bond paper. Clear, black type. "Okay, beastie. Here's an easy one."

Dorothy reached over to the transmat machine and pulled the document feeder tray out from the side. She slid the papers into the tray and the transmat sucked them in with a loud hiss. Lights came on behind the helmet-style visor, illuminating a boxlike compartment. As the pages fluttered onto a platform in the compartment, letter-size sheets of lead foil were interleaved between the three sheets of the document. It seemed rather like making a sandwich for the discriminating palate of a connoisseur in atomic weights.

When the Einsteinian Triple Decker was complete, Dorothy punched in the code for Drane Udrai on a keypad that was ergonomically designed—for the fingers of an infant. Then she pressed a touchpad labeled COPY. With a brief prayer to the deity that watched over recalcitrant office equipment, Dorothy pushed START.

A deep thrum rumbled from the interior of the transmat.

The machine emitted a loud beep.

"Good. They're not busy. Do your stuff, beastie."

Long needles of red light stabbed down into the document, moving from side to side, "reading" the molecular structure of each paper fiber, each iota of laser-jet ink. Back and forth the tiny beams ran, forming ever-shifting patterns—a light show in miniature. Dorothy had found it fascinating when she first started. Now it was routine, and she settled back with the latest issue of *IT, The Fashion Magazine for the Young Androgyne.*

A minute later there came another loud beep and the area behind the visor went black. The plastic hood slid back and the transmat beeped three times. A light labeled TRANSMISSION COMPLETED glowed red above the keypad.

With a sigh of relief, Dorothy pulled the document out of the compartment. All the pages were there. The lead foil was intact. Dorothy patted the machine on its metal carapace. "Attaboy. Keep it up and I'll see you get more deuterium in your diet. Here's the next."

The document was a twenty-pager, bearing the note "Send original, do not copy." It was going to a legal office in New York.

"Someone wants to tempt fate," she muttered as she shunted the weighty tome into the document feeder.

The transmat dutifully sucked it in and interleaved the lead foil between each of the twenty pages. She pushed the touchpad marked ORIGINAL. The location code, and START. All went as before, and Dorothy absorbed herself in her mag's lead fashion article, "The new look is SHAPELESS! Ambiguous dressing adds that sense of mystery to your style!"

The phone rang.

"Mail Room."

"Is this Swanson and Higginbottom?" asked a querulous, nasal female voice.

"Yes, it is. Can I help you?"

"This is the Drane Udrai Insurance Company. Did you just try to transmat something to us?"

"Yes, we did." In matters possibly requiring diplomacy, Dorothy preferred to use the corporational "we."

"Well, all we got was a pile of ashes."

Dorothy's heart sank and her mind raced. "Uh, maybe it was the speed. What speed does your machine receive at? Three, four and a half, or six minutes?"

"Speed? Well, I don't know . . . "

Dorothy felt the usual unholy smugness that she knew more about transmats than other operators, and the problem was, of course, all *their* fault.

". . . you see, we don't set speeds, honey," the nasal voice came back. "Our machine automatically adjusts itself to all speeds. We usually get them in at thirty seconds. You must have a less sophisticated model. Are you sure you can't send faster?"

Dorothy gritted her teeth. "I was told we had top-of-the-line equipment." *And I suppose you get baby PCs as a Christmas bonus each year*. "No."

"Well, you shouldn't always believe the manufacturer's hype, honey. Now, I'll just reset our machine to Mark One, here, and we'll see if that works. You try sending it again."

"Uh, okay, but it won't be for a while. I'm sending out another long document now."

"It will have to be before four-thirty, honey. I'm leaving then."

"Right." Dorothy hung up before she called the woman babycakes, or something worse.

Dorothy narrowed her eyes at the transmat. "Mark One, eh?" What little esteem she felt for the machine was plummeting rapidly. The transmat beeped three times and the visor opened. Only the foil interleaves were left on the platform. "Good beastie." She sighed. "Now let's try the first one again, and do get it right this time, please?"

Dorothy shoved the previous three pages back into the machine. As the paper zipped inside, she looked up at the clock. It was 4:25. "Well, with any luck—"

The phone rang.

"Is this Swanson and Higginbottom, in Minneapolis?"

"Yes, it is."

"This is the Souforlotz and Getimoff Law Office in New York. We are expecting an important document from your office. Has there been some problem, or delay, or what?"

What! "No, not at all. That document's been sent! Didn't you receive it?"

"No, we haven't."

"But I just sent it! Have you checked with your transmat operator? Perhaps it's still in her—"

"We are standing *at* the transmat machine," the woman on the other end replied testily. "Nothing has come through in the past fifteen minutes."

Oh, shit. "Uhhh . . . perhaps there has been a mistake. I'll try to track it down and call you back."

"Just see if you can send it right away, please."

"Right." Dorothy hung up and immediately made a call.

"Julia, Bond Department."

"Hi, Julia, this is Dorothy in the mail room."

"Hi, did that transmat go okay?"

"Well, no."

"Did it turn into glue like the last time?"

"No, the law office just called and said it never got there at all. It went off into never-never land. Are you sure you gave me the right location code?"

"Damn, I *think* so. I hope it didn't appear in some other office. That was personal info. And that was the original document too, wasn't it?"

Dorothy was grateful that Julia sounded sympathetic. "Yes, it was. I don't suppose you have a usable copy to send?"

"I'll check our files. I knew we should have sent that by overnight mail. I'll look for that number too, and call you back. Bye."

"Bye."

The transmat beeped.

The phone rang.

"Mail Room."

"Dorothy? This is Saul in Property. Did my transmat go yet?"

She checked the row of items on her desk. "Uh, you're about fifth in line."

"Does that mean it will go out tonight?"

"Well, I can't promise it. The transmat seems to be acting up and—"

"Look, that's really a rush job. Can you maybe move it up on the list?"

"Saul, every document in the line is a rush. If you want to fight with the people ahead of you, be my guest, but I really don't have authority to—"

"I'll get back to you." He hung up.

Dorothy sighed and tried to remember where she was before the flurry began. The transmat's visor was up. Dorothy pulled out the little three-page document, which seemed blessedly still intact. She looked at the clock. It was 4:35. *Well, they ought to have it this time.*

The phone rang.

"Mail Room."

"Swanson and Higginbottom? This is Drane Udrai again. We received your transmat—"

"Oh, good."

"But they're all garbled. I can't read a word on them."

"Oh, no. Should I sent them again?"

"Don't bother, honey. I think our machines are just plain incompatible. Have your people send it some other way. I'm getting out of here. Bye."

"Yeah." Dorothy scrawled CAN'T SEND across the

cover sheet and set the three pages aside. "That's one way to solve the problem."

She turned to the next project in the line. *Oh, God.* It was one of those jobs for which the transmat was invented—a sample of a client's product. It was soft and pinkish and amorphous in shape. According to the letter accompanying the object, it was some sort of experimental "bioplastic" medical device—perhaps a substitute for a transplanted organ. Dorothy couldn't tell for sure from the obfuscatory prose. It had to go to the S&H affiliate in London, England.

"Beastie, if this goes through, it will be a miracle."

Dorothy opened the visor and placed the cover letter on the platform, then the "thing" on top of it. In order to line up the object precisely, Dorothy had to put her head partway into the compartment. On the back wall of the compartment was a small, red plaque. Dorothy moved her head in further to read its message. The tiny print read, in Japanese, Chinese, German, and English: DO NOT, UNDER ANY CIRCUMSTANCES, PLACE HEAD, HANDS, OR OTHER PART OF THE BODY OVER THE TRANSMITTING PLATFORM. NEVER ATTEMPT TO SEND LIVING MATTER OF ANY KIND.

"All right. No leaving Fluffy in the transmat machine."

Dorothy suddenly realized her head was directly over the transmitting platform. She jerked herself out, banging her head on the edge of the compartment.

With the anger of one who has just been assaulted by an inanimate object, Dorothy slammed the visor shut. She rubbed her abused scalp and punched in the long, overseas transmission code.

More long, red needles stabbed into the compartment, this time forming a cubical grid around the object. The light played over its surface, recording its size, shape, and molecular composition. By the laser illumination, Dorothy saw a strand of her dark hair lying across the top of the object.

"Well, hair isn't living matter, exactly, so I'm not breaking any rules."

Wearily, she sat and turned back to her magazine. She was particularly intrigued by one ad: "Bored with your ordinary face? Use Presto-Chango™ latex appliances for that strikingly *different* appearance they'll swear you were born with!"

The phone rang.

"Mail Room."

"Dorothy, this is Saul. I just spoke to Sam. He wants that transmat of mine out ASAP, you understand?"

"Oh." Sam Aires was the head honcho of the office. He was also a walking emotional land mine—one false step with him and ka-blooey. "All right. When does it absolutely have to be there?"

"Yesterday."

"Very funny, Saul."

"I'm not joking. Our people in Princeton needed that information yesterday for a presentation tomorrow. As it is, we probably won't get the account, but at least we can keep our team from looking like idiots, all right?"

"Gotcha. I'll put it next in line."

"You do that." He hung up.

Dorothy sighed and looked at the clock. It was

5:10. The transmat was still humming and flashing, sending its burden to merrie olde England. Suddenly Dorothy realized she had forgotten to reset the machine to COPY from ORIGINAL. Blast. She picked up the phone and dialed.

"International and Marine."

"Bernice? This is Dorothy."

"Hi, Dorothy. Has my transmat gone to London yet?"

"Yes, it's on its way."

"Oh, good."

"Quite literally. I accidentally sent the original. Is that all right? I hope that isn't the only sample you have."

"Oh, dear, dear. Well. I suppose we can just have them send it back. I have to talk to them tomorrow anyway. So long as it gets there, don't worry about it, Dorothy."

"Thank you." Dorothy breathed in relief.

"No problem. Bye."

Dorothy hung up and looked back at the transmat. It was still sending. *C'mon, c'mon,* she grumbled, tapping her fingers on her desk.

The phone rang.

"Mail Room." Dorothy was unable to completely keep the irritation from her voice.

A smooth male voice replied, "Hello, is this Swanson—"

"Yes, this is Swanson and Higginbottom. Can I help you?"

"Well," said the insinuating voice, "I think it is I who can help you."

"What?" *I don't need a jerk obscene phone call. Not now.*

"This is Swamp and McCartney . . . "

Our big competitors? Why are they calling? "Yes?"

"We just received a stack of legal forms that we have traced back to your office. The information in them is kind of personal, and I have no indication of whose attention they were to be addressed to."

Ohgodohgodohgod. "Uh . . . "

"Would I be correct in assuming these might have been sent to our office by mistake?"

"Yes! Yes! A mistake! A simple mistake! Uh, please disregard them. Please!"

"They'll go right into my circular file, I promise," said the smoothie. "I won't tell a soul. But next time you might want to check your location a little better before you send, hmm?"

"Right." Dorothy threw the receiver back onto the phonebox and stared at it. *There goes my job. There goes my career. Please, god, don't let Sam find out. Let me be wrong and let that fellow have been an honest chap who will dump the papers like he said. What am I going to tell Julia?*

The phone rang.

"Mail Room," Dorothy said mournfully.

"Dorothy, this is Julia. Listen, pulling together a copy of that document would take a long time. It'd be a lot easier to find out where the original went. I looked up the location code—did I give you 1174 or 1175?"

"I don't remember, Julia, it was written on the top page of the document."

"Which is now gone. I get it. It should have gone to 1175. If it went to 1174, that's Standard Insurance, and they might be able to send it back to us or on to the law office. I sure hope it didn't go to 1176—that's Swamp and McCartney. They'd just love to do their worst with some of that info."

"Oh. Yeah."

"You okay, Dorothy? You sound a little shaky."

"Oh, just rushed, that's all."

"So check with Standard and see if they got it, okay?"

"Okay."

Julia hung up.

Dorothy tried not to scream. *What now? What now? Why didn't I tell her? I don't even know whose mistake it was so I don't know who to yell at.*

The transmat beeped and Dorothy nearly jumped off her chair. Getting control of herself, she flipped open the visor and then remembered there was nothing to remove. She dropped heavily back in the chair and grabbed Saul's report, trying not to think of how many ways she could be drawn and quartered if the management found out about the missing papers.

She shoved the papers in the feeder swiftly, but neatly. This time she was careful to push COPY before going for the location code. She punched in the number for Princeton and sat down, burying her head in her arms.

The phone rang.

"Shut up!"

It rang again.

"Mail Room!" she answered.

"Er, excuse me," said a male voice with a British accent, "is this Swanson and Higginbottom in the States?"

"Yes it is," said Dorothy with mingled delight and dread. Ordinarily she loved listening to English accents. It was part of the reason she had applied to Lloyds U. But now . . .

"Did you just send to us . . . er, something for our Marine Department?"

"Yes, I did. Didn't it come through all right?"

"The letter came through just fine but—look here, if this is someone's idea of a joke, it just isn't funny."

"Joke? What do you mean? It's a sample of a client's product—some sort of medical technology. Didn't the letter explain that? Did the letter come through garbled?"

"It isn't the *letter* at all. It's what's on top of it. That blob of brown goop that looks like . . . well, I don't care to say what it looks like. If that's an example of 'medical technology,' I—hang on, it's moving."

"Moving?"

"Crikey, it's crawling out—one moment." There came the sound of the receiver being dropped and the caller stepped away. Dorothy heard grunts and the sound of something banging on metal and wood. Then there came a distinct scream.

Dorothy threw the phone down and wondered frantically what to do. *Should I call Scotland Yard? What would I tell them? Do they take this sort of job? Do they take calls from crazy Americans who think they've just murdered someone by transmatting a hair?* She could see the headlines in the London *Star*:

IT CRAWLED OUT OF THE TRANSMAT MACHINE! BROWN BLOB COMMITS GRISLY MURDER! CIA PLOT SUSPECTED! Dorothy rubbed her face and wished she could disappear under the desk.

The transmat beeped.

Dorothy jumped. The visor automatically flipped open and the pages of Saul's report came fluttering out of the machine.

"Now what?" Dorothy bent and picked up the errant pages and then looked at the machine. An angry red error light was flashing over the keypad. "Just what I need."

The phone rang.

"Go away!"

It rang again. Dorothy let it ring two more times before she reluctantly picked it up.

"Mail Room."

"This is Saul. Princeton just called. They still haven't gotten that report yet."

"No. I know. There's something wrong with the machine."

"Well, can you fix it?"

"I don't know."

"Call the service person."

"It's after hours, Saul. A servicer couldn't be here until tomorrow. In the afternoon. If we're lucky."

"Oh, God. Look just get that thing out, I don't care how you do it." His receiver slammed off.

Directing every curse and obscenity she knew at the telephone, Dorothy began searching her desk for the manual on the transmat. She found it in the little-used drawer and wearily flipped it open. Under the section labeled "Troubleshooting" were two entries. "1. Check to see that main unit is plugged into wall socket. 2. Call customer service representative."

"Great." She looked up at the clock. It was 5:30. She flipped idly through the rest of the manual. *I shoulda stayed in bed this morning. I just knew it.*

She came across the schematics for the boards that were the transmat's brains. "Caution," read a note at the bottom of the page, "reversing of wires F and G in area 6 will result in transposition of transmitted matter to tachyons. Be certain that this configuration is correctly wired before operating machinery." A wild thought burst into Dorothy's insane, stress-induced mood.

Tachyons, thought Dorothy. From her introduction to physics class, she knew that tachyons spin backward in time. *So. Want it yesterday, do you, Saul?*

Dorothy had friends at school who were computer hardware wizards. It was no problem to call out for a little general advice—although it meant she had to agree to dates with a couple of them. She found a screwdriver and removed a panel in the back of the transmat. On the panel was another small, red plaque on which was inscribed: TAMPERING WITH EQUIPMENT BY NONAUTHORIZED PERSONS MAY RESULT IN PROSECUTION. DO NOT REMOVE.

"Come and get me."

She easily found the appropriate chip board and swapped the relevant wires. She selected the "delay transmission" feature on the transmat and set it to twenty-four hours. She replaced the pages of the report, properly interleaved, back onto the platform.

With unholy glee, she punched in Princeton's number and pushed START. Then she ducked behind the cubical wall and waited, as the transmat wailed and the most amazing light patterns played on the ceiling.

Dorothy blinked and she was standing at her desk. She looked at the clock. It was 4:50. She looked back at her desk. It was absolutely clear, except for one envelope. The transmat still stood by the desk, but it was subtly different—Dorothy was not sure in what way. As she looked around, Dorothy had the feeling many things were different. It was peaceful. Too peaceful.

The door to the mail room burst open and her coworker Patsy bustled in. She gave Dorothy an embarrassed smile. "Forgot my hat. Look, I feel bad about you're not being invited to the champagne celebration."

"Celebration?"

"For that big account we just landed this afternoon. It's really tacky how they're treating you. I mean, it's not like you were caught embezzling, or anything. Well, like I said, wherever you go I wish you the best of luck. Keep in touch, okay?"

"Yeah, okay," Dorothy murmured, mystified, as Patsy hurried out the door. She let her gaze fall back to the envelope on her desk. A sliver of pink showed through the cellophane window.

She tore open the envelope and scanned the note it contained. "Atten: Head of Work-Study Program, Adams High School . . . Termination with prejudice . . . " read the pink slip, " . . . uncooperative behavior . . . tampering with office machinery . . . "

Dorothy crumpled the pink slip and collapsed into the chair.

"Ingrates!" she wailed before the tears began to fill up her eyes. She stared at the desk—and realization set in. "If there are no transmats to send, the embarrassing legal papers will not have gone to Swamp and McCartney. And the Follicle Monster won't have slimed that poor fellow in London. It could be worse, couldn't it, beastie?"

The transmat swiveled on its wheels until its visor faced her. "Please remain seated, Miss Wangsrupt," it said in a metallic warble.

She sat.

The phone rang.

Dorothy froze. Slowly she reached out and picked up the receiver. "Mail Room," she whispered.

"Miss Wangsrupt?" The voice was male, crisp and businesslike.

"Yes. Who—?"

"This is Transpace Electronics. It is very important that we speak with you."

"Yes?"

"We understand you may be feeling somewhat disoriented and upset, Miss Wangsrupt. Nonetheless, the matter of your tampering with our equipment is very serious."

"Oh." Dorothy swallowed hard.

The transmat beeped and its "receiving" lights flashed.

"Please note the incoming transmission, Miss Wangsrupt."

The visor opened and a long piece of paper rolled

out. Dorothy reached over and took it, the page rattling as her hand shook. It was the front page of the Business section of the Minneapolis *Stribune*. In the lower right corner was the headline TRANSPACE EQUIPMENT PLANT DESTROYED IN $10,000,000 BLAZE. And beneath that, DISGRUNTLED STUDENT WORKER SUSPECTED OF ARSON. The article was accompanied by two photos: one of a building afire, the other of a begrimed Dorothy being led away in cuffs.

Dorothy had to admit the thought had occurred to her. She noted the date on the paper. It was May 24, 2041. Two weeks in the future. Trying to put some steel in her voice, she said, "You can't have me arrested for something I haven't done yet."

"Assuredly not, Miss Wangsrupt. However, there is a substantial penalty for unlawful tampering."

"You . . . how did you know?"

The transmat warbled, "I am equipped with temporal readjustment detectors."

The phone voice continued, "Miss Wangsrupt, your little stunt set off alarms all over our office, as well as in the receiving transmat in Princeton."

"I see. So. I'm to be punished?"

A dry chuckle crackled in the receiver. "Some might call it that, Miss Wangsrupt. We would like to make you an offer. A scholarship in our orbital engineering training labs, say, with a guaranteed position afterward in our R and D Department, as, say, an ergonomics consultant. We felt an appropriate starting salary might be—" He named a figure five times what she might have expected. Dorothy held tight control over her jaw muscles lest she chin the floor.

"Considering our offer? I will say that we need your decision now, Miss Wangsrupt. Otherwise, well, other action might have to be taken."

Dorothy stared at the transmat machine. Could the thing that had been the nemesis of her career now be its savior? She remembered all the frustrating, aggravating, infuriating hours she had spent. She turned back to the receiver.

"Miss Wangsrupt?"

"Sir. I have decided to give you the best ergonomic advice I can . . . for free. I can sum it up in one sentence. *Make things that work the way they're supposed to and don't foist them on the public until they do.*" She slammed the receiver down.

The transmat wailed. "Warning! Warning! Tachyon reception detected! Possible timeline alteration imminent! Warning! Warning!"

Lights flashed all over its carapace and the transmat shuddered, its visor slapping up and down. It gave a final shake and the visor shot open.

A long piece of paper fluttered out. It glowed red for a few moments, then settled down to a natural, newspaperlike appearance. Dorothy picked it up. It was the front page of the Business section of the *Stribune*. In the lower left corner was an article headed: RELIABLE TRANS/FAX UNVEILS NEW PRODUCT. "President Dorothy Wangsrupt makes tantalizing promises with her faster-than-instantaneous transmat equipment. If her marketing briefs hold a shred of truth, Reliable Trans/Fax will be giving every other company in the field a run for their money, if not pronouncements of doom."

The accompanying photo with the article showed Dorothy seated in an elegant office. The caption read, "President Wangsrupt of RTF in her new branch office in Olympus View, Mars."

Scrawled across the article were the words "Way to go, girl!" in her own handwriting. The date on the paper was June 1, 2051—ten years ahead.

Dorothy frowned. The arrival of the first paper hadn't caused as much hoopla on the transmat. She compared the page with the one sent by Transpace. There was a subtle difference in the layout and typeface. Inspecting the first newssheet carefully, Dorothy came across the tiny letters "©Spaceport Novelty Company."

Dorothy crumpled the bogus newspaper and looked at the transmat. "Clever. You don't know how I did it, but you hoped I would tell you. You knew it was possible, but your R and D boys couldn't figure it out. You set alarms, planted hints, and waited for someone to do what you couldn't. Well, congratulations. This is the end of an annoying friendship and the beginning of a brilliant career—although a slightly different one than I'd planned."

She stood and gathered her things.

"Please sit down," burbled the transmat.

"Please get stuffed," said Dorothy, ramming the fake *Stribune* into the transmat. She slammed the visor shut and punched in Transpace's code number and pressed SEND. Then, to the tune of the transmat chugging and choking, she stepped onto the path to a bright and prosperous future.

8

EAR

Jane Yolen

Jily put on her Ear and sighed. The world went from awful silence to the pounding rhythms she loved. Without the Ear she was locked into her own thoughts and the few colors her eyes could pick out. But with the Ear she felt truly connected to the world.

"Bye, Ma!" she called in her thick voice, and waved.

Earless, her mother never looked up as Jily ran out the door.

The night was ablaze with sound and the winking of lights up and down the street. Everything was sending messages that she was never able to hear during the day in school when she was without her Ear. Jily touched the skin-colored Ear and smiled.

Sanya and Feeny met her at the corner, under the sallow crooning light. Sanya's new Ear was a particularly odious shade of green, the hottest color but not good on her. Jily debated whether to say anything, then decided to keep silent. Sanya was too new a friend for her to chance honesty. Maybe later. Maybe when the music began. Maybe then she might have the nerve to tell Sanya how awful the green Ear was.

"Swing!" Jily called out to them.

"Low!" they returned. With their Ears, they could hear the greetings.

Arms linked, they walked down the noise-filled street.

The first club they came to, The Low Down, was too dark and too quiet for Jily's taste, but Sanya, with her new terrible green Ear, insisted on staying and sampling everything.

Showing off, Jily thought, but kept it to herself.

There was a gray bar in the corner and the drinks sold were nonalkie of course, but with their Ears, they could pick up all the sub-lime messages, which made everything fine. The Olds were the only ones who still needed alkie to be high. And anyway, being *low* was the thing now.

Jily bent over and put her Ear near the drinks, grubbing on the sounds.

"Soooooo smooooth," whispered one of the drinks, its voice clear. "Soooooo smooooth."

The next glass bubbled. "Makes you smiiiiile." By pushing the two glasses close together, Jily could hear them at the same time, a cheery duet. She ordered them both.

When she'd finished and looked up, Sanya was dancing slowly by herself on the tiny handkerchief-size dance floor, turning round and round, her arms spread wide. What she was hearing Jily didn't know because there was no band. *Maybe*, she thought, maybe the green Ear picks up something even lower. But she didn't ask. She didn't even want to mention the green Ear yet.

Feeny was standing at the other end of the gray bar staring at a couple of guys. They were Earless. Jily knew Earless never came into the clubs, just as Olds never did.

She walked over to Feeny and fitted her arm over Feeny's shoulder, whispering right into her Ear, something they had done ever since they had become best friends, turning twelve on the exact same day and getting their Ears together. "How *can* they?"

Feeny turned, whispered back, tickling Jily's Ear with her breath, the words coming out thick and thin, thick and thin, not at all clear like the voices from the drinks. "I heard about it at school. It's new. It's low. Coming out and grubbing Earless. It's called Kellering. And they have a sticker too. *Making the past the future.* Don't you think that's kind of cute?"

"I think that's kind of sick," Jily said. "And it's making them Old."

"Well, I think they're cute," Feeny said. "Let's ask them to dance."

"There's no band," Jily whispered furiously. "And even if there were, they couldn't hear without Ears."

Feeny shrugged and peeled away from Jily's imprisoning arm. She went up to one of the guys and pulled on his long straight black pigtail. Then she waggled her fingers. He nodded and they leaned forward, shoulders touching, to stare down at the floor, and slowly they began to dance The Slope. Even without music, he seemed to have rhythm, Jily thought. Even without an Ear.

Jily bit her lip. *Still—he was Earless! How could he!* She knew she'd just die at night on the street without her Ear. Just shrivel up and become an Old all at once. Being Earless meant being Ancient. Like in the far back days when no one had Ears and everyone was deaf from the loud music and the vid ads. Till the Townshend Law was passed, named after the old rocker who'd first admitted losing his hearing. And then everyone in junior high, everyone twelve years old, was issued an Ear to be worn only out of school. At night. On the streets. The Ears that gave new life and made the world real again. And low.

The other guy, redheaded with a star map of freckles across his nose, saw Jily. He waggled his fingers, an invitation to dance. She pointed at her Ear and shook her head, turning her back on him, refusing to sign properly because *she*, after all, was wearing an Ear.

When she glanced back over her shoulder, he was dancing with Sanya, not touching, fingertips apart, doing a dance Jily couldn't identify. Sanya's green Ear seemed almost alive. It was the color of pond scum, the color of bile. Jily's cat had sicked up something that color once. Jily hated it and closed her eyes, trying to hear what Sanya was hearing. She heard feet scuffling and some low giggles from the corner and the coy whispering of the drinks lined up on the gray bar. *So smoooooooth. Makes you smiiiiiiiiile. Licking goooooood.*

"I'm going!" she called, not even turning her face

to her friends, an insult of the worst order, and she didn't even care. If they heard, they didn't bother to answer.

—·—

Outside her Ear picked up every loud, comforting noise, grinding the messages into her skull. Trucks rattled by calling out *Heavy load, watch out!* The undergrounds grumbled ceaselessly, *Next stop Central,* when they were going north, *Next stop Market* when they were southbound. Chattering signs assailed her from the shops.

She found another club down the block, The Lower Depths, and turned in, somehow thankful to have the noise of the street muffled in the band's crankings. It was a dark club featuring a Cyber Band, with its players fully chipped and plugged into their instruments. The only light was on the stage and the bass player was really low, his hair looking as if it were electric itself, black and kinky, and standing up around his head like the rays of a black sun. The green plug lines were set into his forehead in their puckered sockets. It was the same green as Sanya's Ear and for a moment Jily closed her eyes.

She moved forward onto the dance floor and to the right side of the stage to get as close to the band as possible. The lights on stage changed and she saw his plug lines weren't green at all, more a mellow yellow, and that made her smile. She let herself ground in his lows. She let the sounds wash over her, tumbling her in their waves, nearly drowning her. It was how she loved it most, leaving her no room to think, only room to feel. She didn't want to think anyway, about Sanya and Feeny back in the quiet club with the gray bar and its drinks whispering messages. Rather she would give herself up to the band's deep groundings, the great tidal pull of noise.

Someone tapped her on the shoulder. When she turned, swimming up from the music, she could see by the reflected light from the stage that it was the redheaded guy, the one without the Ear, only in the light his red hair looked almost orange, almost glowing. He cupped his hand to the side of his head, which meant he wanted to talk.

Jily shook her head, meaning *No talking. Not here. Not now. Not with the music still washing through me.*

But when he insisted, striking himself over the temples, the signal that no one was allowed to ignore, all her fifteen years of training punctured the wall of music and dragged her through. She nodded and followed him to the door. They'd speak outside where there was light to read the signs by, where she wouldn't be tempted by the music.

As she walked up the stairs, she called him names in her head. Horrible names, like derb and tweep. He was an Earless gink, she thought fiercely, making moves on her and forcing her up into the light. Still, by all the rules she grew up with, she knew she had to at least listen to him, if only for the time it took her to tell him to grub off.

Once they were outside, she took out her Ear and stuffed it into her jacket pocket.

"Grub off!" her hands shouted at him. "This is my Ear time. Leave me be, gink." The sign for *gink* was cramped and ugly.

He only grinned at the insult, and the constellations of freckles over his nose seemed to wink. His hands spoke quietly of a better sound, a lower sound, a sound they could share.

"You're an Earless gink," she retorted, her fingers picking at her ear and cramping again to show her utter disdain, though she did wonder how he could seem so happy despite not wearing an Ear. The Olds never really seemed happy Earless. You had to give up your Ear at thirty. Something to do with nerve damage and ruptured DNA or corrupted DNA. Something like that. She'd learned it at school. Or at least it was taught there.

He made the quiet sign again for lower sound and grinned.

She might have asked him where, but just then she saw Sanya and Feeny out by another streetlight with the black-haired guy. The three of them were holding hands. Hand in hand in hand.

"Sanya!" she called out, and signed the name as well.

Sanya didn't respond, didn't even turn toward her. It was then she realized that the green Ear was gone.

"What have you done to them?" she signed furiously at the redhead. "Why are they Earless? Sanya's Ear was new. And even if it *was* an awful green, she'd never take it off. Not at night. Not the first night she had it on."

He only smiled and waggled back an innocuous, "Ask her yourself."

She flipped him the grub-off sign and pointedly took the Ear from her pocket, making a big fuss about putting it back in.

Just then a big truck barreled by, rattling its monotonous *Heavy load* warning, and Jily turned away.

She went back down into The Lower Depths alone, leaving the two boys and her two best friends Earless in the street above. But somehow this time the sound in the club dragged her down. She'd lost the rhythm, lost the wonderful feeling of drowning in the sound. The bass player looked much older than she'd first thought. Maybe even closing in on thirty. Almost an Old. Of course he didn't need an Ear. He was a musician. He was chipped and plugged for as long as he lasted. Some even lasted to thirty-five before they died, before the Resurrection Men got their body parts. But they had sound all that time. And they never had to get Old and go Earless forever.

The drinks at the bar chittered away. The music ground on. But Jily couldn't stop thinking about Sanya and Feeny out on the street. Earless. After another twenty minutes, she left the club. But the street was empty. Sanya and Feeny and the two guys were long gone.

The next day at school both Sanya and Feeny were absent, and so Jily had no one to hand-chat with. She hung around the edges of a couple of the girl groups, and even sidled up to watch the flying fingers of one of the couples. But it was as if they were all signing some mysterious language she'd never learned.

Slowly she drifted back into the classroom, sat down at her desk, and booted up a favorite old novel. She was partway to scrolling the first chapter when the bell flashed and everyone returned, forcing her to dump the novel and get online with the teacher. After an hour, the phosphor words made her head ache. At school's end she had a raging migraine.

Walking home alone, she wondered if she should report Sanya and Feeny missing. Maybe she had been the last one to see them alive. *Maybe,* she thought suddenly, *maybe those weren't boys at all but murderers. Slavers. True, there was hardly any crime anymore, but . . .*

They were waiting for her at home, talking animatedly with her mother, finger on finger. Sanya wasn't wearing her bilious green Ear, but of course it was too early in the day for that.

"Where *were* you?" Jily signed frantically, not sure if she was angry with them, or relieved.

"They were Earless in Gaza," her mother spelled out.

What she said made no sense, but like many of the things her mother said, it probably referred to some book or other. Olds read *books*, not phosphor. *Figure Olds!* she thought savagely.

"We had our parents' permission," Sanya signed. "We didn't need yours."

Trying to soften Sanya's remarks, Feeny added,

"We were at this *other* school. Where they read books. And discuss offline with real teachers. And . . . "

Jily made a face. It all suddenly made terrible sense to her. Those two Earless ginks weren't just kids trying out a new style, looking for a new Low. They were part of that movement, that Kellering. And it wasn't just a fun thing! *Oh, no!* she thought. *They really do want to make the past the future.* She grimaced. *In the past, only the Olds had fun and the kids were Earless.*

"So you want to make the past the future!" she said to Sanya and Feeny suddenly, giving the extra little wrist twist that told them just what she *really* thought about the idea. Telling them without words, just motions, something signing did even better than the thick words, what ginks they both were. "Those guys were some kind of missionaries. Out to collect their quota of converts. And you two fell for it. Well, not me. I'm going to wear my Ear till the DNA twists!"

Sanya reached into her pocket and pulled out the bilious green Ear. "I don't want this anymore. And I don't know who else to give it to." Her fingers, snapping out the message, added a little pinkie flip that meant *or anyone else I'd do this to.*

"I don't want your cast-off," Jily shouted in her thick voice. "I don't want your stupid green sick-up color Ear." And though no one could hear her, they all knew what she meant because she accompanied her words with a slap on Sanya's wrist that was so hard, the green Ear sailed into the air, spun over twice, and fell behind the couch.

Sanya held out her wrist, bright red from the slap, and showed it to Feeny, but she was smiling.

Feeny put her arm around Sanya's shoulder and turned her toward the door. They walked out that way, with Feeny's arm draped like a shawl around Sanya. The door closed silently behind them.

Jily sat the rest of the day in her room, refusing even to come out for dinner, refusing to do her homework, refusing even to turn on the computer. She let the silence, heavy as any noise, envelop her.

As night crept into her room on silent paws, she got up, patting the pocket where her Ear was waiting.

In the living room, she found the green Ear, covering it quickly with her hand so she didn't have to look at the color.

Once in the street, she jammed the green Ear in her left, her own Ear in her right. The sudden noise of the street was so loud, she almost passed out.

Squaring her shoulders, she stared defiantly at a truck rattling by. "If it's too loud," she shouted in her thick voice, startling two pigeons off a garbage can, "then you're too old!"

Then with the pounding messages of trucks and stop lights and shop windows and subways growling into her from both Ears, drowning out her sorrow, drowning out her fear, drowning out the last of her thoughts, she danced and sang down the street into the ever-young night.

9

THE LAST OUT

Resa Nelson and David Alexander Smith

Every time you come back to Fenway Park, thought reserve catcher Marty Warden, guiding his car over the pontoon-supported surface of Yawkey Causeway, it's sunk a little deeper into the ocean. After today's game, no one will ever come here anymore.

The park loomed ahead, a green and orange fortress surrounded on three sides by the encroaching harbor. Beyond it, the Downtown Ring's hodgepodge of towers gleamed. Boston was becoming islands among the wreckage.

After the dry sun outside, the Red Sox clubhouse was moist and cool. As he had done every game day for the last fourteen years, Marty stripped and lowered himself into the whirlpool's burbling heat, his arms draped over the sides, his head tilted back. When his calf muscles were loose, he reached into the scalding water and massaged each kneecap, sliding the bone around in its bag of skin until it fit with the least pain.

Setting himself on the edge of the whirlpool, Marty dried his legs, then wrapped Ace bandages around them, ankle to groin, softly at first and then gradually tighter. That done, he walked naked to the trainer's room, where Roger Bryson covered the bandages with white adhesive tape until Marty looked like the victim of a ski accident.

"How they feel today?" asked Bryson, deftly slicing tape with his thumbnail.

"Like hot needles." Marty gazed down at his toes so far removed from his body.

"The chips keep splintering," the pudgy trainer replied apologetically. "At least this is the final game of the season. After today you can relax."

"Sure." Marty waddled over to his locker. "After today I can relax."

He dressed, starting with his jock and the plastic cup over it, then pulling on his uniform pants and settling the red stirrups, smoothing the trousers against his adhesive tape.

"Warden, you were late today," said Royal O'Connor behind him.

"Got a speeding ticket," grumbled Marty, turning to greet his manager. "Guy didn't recognize me. Can you believe it?"

O'Connor shrugged, squinting as if his reserve catcher were a fly ball twisting foul. "What can you give me today?"

"One at-bat."

The skipper frowned. "Nothing behind the plate, not even in the ninth?"

"The knees hurt real bad today, Royal. I can't bend. But I can give you one truly fine at-bat."

O'Connor shoved another clump of his chewing tobacco into his mouth, working it into a brown ball that bulged his cheek. He spat neatly between the gap in his front teeth and pinged a half-full beer can into the trash. "I'll get you one."

"Don't do it for me."

"Why not?" demanded O'Connor. "You're my oldest friend. We can't win the pennant if we're twenty out with one to play."

"That ain't it, Royal, and you know it." To rest his knees, Marty leaned against the whirlpool. "Play the best you got, Royal. You always gotta put the best on the field."

The Red Sox skipper listened patiently, a faint grin on his face. He spat through his teeth again. "Bum wheels or no, Warden, you can still drive the baseball deep. That's what kept you in the league these last three seasons. Might as well go out in style, right?"

"Royal, why are they tearing Fenway down? The ballpark looks fine to me."

"Warden, it'll look solid until they blow it apart. The rot is inside—inside the beams, in the concrete that keeps falling. It's too risky to stay here. Besides, an indoor stadium's a better year-round ballfield."

Marty massaged his right shoulder, his powerful fingers working out the knots of tension he always felt before game time. "Life goes on, Royal. The Sox will play next season."

"I won't." O'Connor spat at the beer can.

"Why, Royal?" Shocked, Marty sagged against the

whirlpool. "You've got a lot of good years left. Managers don't get bum wheels. Why do you want to quit?"

"Tell me, Warden, do you *like* hitting with a vidcamera like a miniature blimp floating six feet over the pitcher's head and watching you?" O'Connor bit into his chaw and jammed it from one cheek to the other. "Do you *like* playing in vacant stands in a sinking quagmire?"

"It's going to be full today, Royal. Today's game's sold out."

"And who bought tickets?" The manager snorted and spat. "Targives and other aliens from beyond the Loophole who want to see our quaint ritual before it becomes extinct. Ghouls who come to bury the corpse of a dead stadium. People who like the *nostalgia* of clean baseball. You ever watch open-league stuff?"

"No." Marty cracked his knuckles. "Six-hundred-foot home runs, hundred-and-fifty-mile fastballs, that ain't baseball. Not when the players are jacked and augged like those guys are."

"Wave of the future, Warden." Royal shrugged. "Faster, higher, stronger. People don't want clean ball anymore. You've busted your knees for a dying sport."

"What am I supposed to do about it?" Marty flared angrily. "I'm seven years old, blocking the plate. Tommy McGee hits me, tears up my knee." He leaned against the whirlpool. "I'm riding in the ambulance, bein' taken to the hospital 'cause my old man wants to get it cut out and plasticked with that new stuff the Targives invented. They're gettin' ready to knock me out. I'm pushing the mouthpiece away. Can't, I keep sayin'. You fix me, I can't play clean ball ever again. I start crying, bawling." Marty massaged his thigh muscle above his scarred knee and sighed. "Clean baseball can't die, Royal. I spent too much pain livin' it."

His manager clapped him on the back. "Next year it won't be clean, Warden. Two more clubs besides us movin' from clean to open league. That leaves only four left."

"You going with the club?" asked Marty.

"Nah. I don't manage juiced players. I got some dignity, my friend. When you get old, dignity's the only thing you can keep. A man can lose it by playing beyond his days. I ain't gonna do that, Warden. It's best to leave when you still have a choice."

Marty had thought of it in different terms: Get out of the game before you make a fool of yourself. The look in his manager's eyes said that Royal knew—probably had known even before Marty himself. He cleared his throat. "You told anyone yet?"

Royal shook his head. "Not until after the season's over." He resumed his brisk managerial tone as if putting on a topcoat and hat. "I'm going to give you one at-bat today, Warden, and you're going to deliver. Right?"

"Right," answered the catcher, running his fingers over the letters of his locker, his final pregame superstition. As Royal walked away, Marty stared at his nameplate, the memory lingering in his fingertips. "I'll always be a catcher, dammit," he murmured.

For months he had known that, come October, his career would have to end. Finish. He had known it would be hard, but he'd never imagined it would feel so like the slamming of a heavy door. He started to touch his nameplate again, then held back. He couldn't do that twice—wouldn't be right. He'd already gone through his ritual for the last time. Marty rubbed his thumb against his fingers as if to force the feeling into them forever. He wanted to memorize every touch, every sight and smell, every aspect of who he was.

"One last at-bat," Marty promised himself. "And I'll deliver if it kills me."

Fenway's rot showed worst in the tunnel leading onto the field. The concrete underfoot was fissured and fragmented, with mud and mildew seeping into the cracks. Small animals, terrestrial and alien, scurried behind the walls. Now and then the steel beams groaned like wounded elephants, twisting under the stress as the land that held them sank. If I died here, thought Marty, no one would have to bury me. Just wall up either end of the tunnel and let the ferrets eat my bones.

With a sigh, he limped up the dugout steps, smelling the wind, his eyes closed. The late-September air was chill and dry. Sure enough, the tattered American League flag rippled in the wind, blowing out. A well-hit fly ball might carry for a home run.

The roof's supporting beams were rusted and brittle like red lichen, and the grounds crew had filled the foul-territory sinkholes with sand. Still, no matter how the stadium collapsed about it, the playing field itself was a jewel. The grass, thriving on the subsurface moisture, was green and lush. Its soft carpet, spongy with moisture, buoyed his spikes.

Marty strolled toward the cage, the crack of fungoes echoing like logs popping in a fire. He moved slowly. No need to let anyone know how crippled he was.

The centerfield stands were dark green and gray, empty of fans. As the street behind them had fallen away, the city had been forced to condemn the sinking, crumbling bleachers. Now they were fenced off.

When the first pitch came he swung easily, connecting with the sharp sweet crack of perfect timing.

His stroke was still a pure and beautiful movement, almost effortless in its grace, swift and potent. Ball after ball he powered: to left, to center, down the right-field line, practicing his uppercut for the sacrifice fly, his top-hand-over for the grounder to the right side.

In the batting cage, he hit as if he were twenty-two again, his arms and hands moving like pistons and wheels, oiled and friction free. All the while his eyes roved the outfield and stands, as if seeing Fenway for the first time, trying to freeze the memory forever.

When his pitches were done, Marty stepped out of the cage, a creaking old man of thirty-two, his knees and calves pitchforks of agony. He moved slowly back toward the dugout, disguising his pain as nonchalance.

"Hey, Warden," sang out a woman's voice from the box seats behind first base.

"Howdy, Lizbeth. How's the baby?" Smiling, Marty gestured at her police uniform. "You on duty today?"

"Always work the games when I can. The baby's great," Lizbeth Faulkner answered cheerfully. "Bishop twenty-four is throwing out the first ball. I'm his bodyguard." She shivered. "Not that the big bug needs one."

"Oh? Isn't he important?"

"He's important, all right. Most important wog in the Interstellar Port of Boston. He's just too scary fast. Anyone gives him trouble, he'll just eat the sucker. Anyway, I don't want to talk about our resident centauran alien. I've got something for you." She waved some snapshots. "Remember this one?"

"Straight change, low and inside." Marty grinned fondly. "Fenstermacher thought I couldn't keep it fair. Thanks for letting me see it." He handed the photograph back to her.

"No, Marty." She brushed it aside. "I want you to have it. Oh, darn, the bishop's getting restless. He thinks baseball's some kind of sentience test where he gets to make a chili dog out of the losing pitcher."

Marty looked with satisfaction at the photo in his hands, savoring the flight of the ball in his mind. He put it in his back pocket. "Thanks, Lizbeth."

"Sure thing. Bye!"

"Hey, Warden," said Yankee rightfielder Clyde Ramirez behind him as Lizbeth hurried up the aisle.

"What do you say, Clyde?" called Marty, grinning over his shoulder. "Put 'er there."

As they shook hands, Ramirez's shoulder shivered and twitched and he winced. His grip was soft and brief.

Marty's eyes narrowed. "You think Detroit's gonna

do it today, Clyde? Win and shut you guys out of the playoffs?"

"Depends on Betty, my man," answered the Yankee rightfielder. "What's she got?"

"Knuckler and guts." Marty thought of the small wiry woman pitcher who had peppered him with questions when the Sox played in Detroit the previous week. "The little girl don't beat herself, but she's got no heat and no curve. Just that butterfly junk."

Ramirez shook his head and blew a pink bubble. "Wish I'd known that last week." He popped it with his tongue and folded it back into his mouth. "She fanned me twice."

"You'll never get to even things up." Marty laughed, shaking his head. "She won't stick through spring training next year. Real shame. She's playing her last game in the majors, and she's too dazzled to know it. Jeez." He pounded the head of his bat into the soggy dirt.

When the national anthem was completed, Marty settled himself on the bench two spaces away from the water cooler.

Jack Lyons, the Red Sox starting catcher, waited for the bishop to throw out the first ball.

Bishop twenty-four was an alien who resembled a three-meter-long praying mantis. He held the ball lightly in one jointed arm, then his whole body shivered as if being observed under strobe lighting and a sound like a gunshot erupted from Jack's mitt.

The crowd murmured, too surprised even to cheer,

everyone restless and disturbed at this awesome display of mobility.

"Gracious lords Brahma, Shiva, and Vishnu," muttered Scooter Ranshakar to Marty's right as the umpire dusted off home plate. "Never shall I play open baseball. Against such as that demon avatar, we must all forget it."

"Okay, Enrique," Marty exhorted the Sox starting pitcher, who was striding to the mound and snapping up the rosin bag as if it were a lost moneypouch. "Let's see what you got."

Joe Bob Hubbard, the Yankee leadoff hitter, stepped into the batter's box like a fighting rooster. "Enrique, *mi hombre*," Marty murmured as if the Sox pitcher could hear him. "Give me a curve, low and outside."

In came the pitch, breaking down and away from Hubbard's swing with a gorgeous bite, and Marty grinned. "Good stuff, Enrique," he coaxed lovingly. "Another. Inside this time."

While Diego worked his way through the first inning, Marty called each pitch to himself, guessing with Jack, gauging the hitters' strengths and weaknesses. When Enrique Diego had set the New Yorkers down in order, the Sox trotted off the field. Diego stomped toward the dugout with his characteristic intensity and slapped palms with Marty. As was his invariable superstition, he then retreated into the Boston clubhouse while the Red Sox batted.

Jack plopped next to Marty with a satisfied sigh. "Nine strikes, four balls," he said proudly. "You call the same thirteen I did?"

Marty methodically rubbed insect repellent onto his arms and hands. The sinking city had turned the Emerald Necklace into a malarial swamp, a breeding ground for both mosquitoes and myriad alien bugs that carried a dozen diseases, several of them fatal. "You missed two. Ramirez's three-oh and Wingo's one-two."

Jack dried off his neck and throat. "Says you. And why the heck does Enrique want your reaction? *I'm* his catcher now." He threw down the towel.

Marty sighed. "Diego doesn't know you," he explained patiently. "I told you this before. A pitcher and a catcher, they're like an old married couple. You know that. They *understand* each other. Half the time Enrique doesn't even look for the sign, because he already knows what pitch I'm thinking."

"So what? He can read my fingers."

"Kid, Enrique didn't want that dumb three-oh slider any more than I did—you saw how he resettled his cap twice."

"If he didn't like the pitch, why'd he *throw* it?"

Marty pounded the bench. "Because *you're* the boss," he hissed, furious. "Enrique was *respecting* you. He's an eleven-year veteran, hundred and twenty wins in the majors. He's faced Ramirez sixty, seventy times. You've only seen Clyde Ramirez on vid. But he takes your orders, kid, and he doesn't complain."

"Hey, Marty, lighten up." Jack chuckled uneasily. "It's only one game. There's always next year."

"For you, maybe," he snarled. "My first two years, every time I'd call a pitch that got hammered, Cookie Monahan would jump up and down on the mound, screaming like a maniac about how *I* gave up that home run and how *I* lost the game and *I* was costing him a spot on the All-Star team. You ain't seen beans, kid." Marty was angrier than he had meant to become. "Kid, give your pitchers time. They have to know they can trust you with their lives."

Jack leaned back and rested his head against the mildewed concrete wall. "Bull. It's just hitting and fielding, not some mystic experience."

—·—

Binsky doubled to start the home half of the second. As Willie Lovelette came up, Jack unstrapped his shin guards and pulled his bat from the rack.

"Wait." Marty put his hand on Jack's shoulder. "If Willie moves Mel over, lift it to right."

Jack shook his head. "It's not my power zone, you know that. I don't think I can hit it far enough."

"Won't matter. Clyde can't throw today. Send it to right, even if it's short."

"How do you know?"

"I got eyes. I see things."

"Okay, Pops," replied Jack, heading for the on-deck circle. "You've got a knack for these hunches."

"Hunches." Marty sniffed, nettled. "He thinks they're hunches."

Lovelette grounded to second, Binsky advancing to third. "In the air to right, kid," muttered Marty as Jack readied himself in the batter's box, closing his stance so that his feet pointed toward right field.

On the mound, Eyebrows Thornton scowled, the bush over his eyes coming together in a single ferocious hedge. On a two-oh fastball, Jack got the pitch he wanted and golfed it, high and short, toward Clyde Ramirez.

Not much, Marty thought worriedly as the ball gleamed in the blue sky above, accompanied by an effortlessly lifting hummingbird camera. Not much at all.

To gain additional power, Ramirez charged the ball as it settled into his glove, but his weak throw sailed high and bounced once as Binsky slid in easily to score the game's first run.

"*Gracias, amigo Hack,*" said Enrique Diego jauntily as the teams changed sides to start the third.

"*De nada, Enrique,*" replied Jack with a grin.

On the Green Monster's manual scoreboard, other games were being posted with painted cards, the same way it had been done for a hundred fifty years. The Tigers were losing, three-zip, but Betty Simmons was still on the mound.

In the third, Diego's control briefly deserted him. "Change," Marty muttered from the dugout as Jack squatted, giving Enrique the signs. "Straight change-up."

Diego shook off Jack, who signed again. With a disdainful, irritated headshake, Diego rejected this choice also.

Go to the mound, kid, thought Marty. When he shakes you, go to the mound. He wants to throw smoke and you can't let him. But Jack was already putting down a sign, and Diego, nodding, was into his windup.

Sitting on the fastball, Clyde Ramirez ripped it into the gap in left center for an easy standup double.

"Damn!" Marty slapped the bench in frustration. "Use your *head*, kid."

Calling time, Jack strolled to the mound, as slowly as a youth ordered to clean up his room. "That's right, kid," Marty approved with a smile. "It's not what *you* say that counts, it's what *he* says to himself while you're on your way there."

A few pitches later, hoping to take advantage of Diego's wildness, Ramirez and Fredericks broke in a double steal. They had a huge jump—Enrique had forgotten all about the runners—but Jack reacted like a jungle cat. Snaring the ball, he whipped it on a beeline into Desmoulins's waiting glove to tag Ramirez out and end the inning.

"What an arm," Marty murmured, impressed.

Diego's troubles continued in the fourth. After two outs, he walked Sanchez and ran the count to two and two against Ray Jones. "Big sweeping lollipop curve," Marty entreated.

In came the pitch, fat and juicy, then breaking perfectly at just the right moment—an exquisite pitch.

Terrific, kid, Marty applauded to himself.

Stepping across the plate, Jones crushed it, so high and deep that Mel Binsky in left didn't even take his hands off his knees. The ball soared over the warped and discolored Green Monster toward the canal that had been the Massachusetts Turnpike.

On the telemonitor in center field, the ball expanded like a globe, then shrank, and the hummingbird camera zoomed in on the teenagers patrolling the

Pike. A towhead dove from her Boston whaler, snaring the ball before it and she both splashed into the water. She surfaced, the ball lodged firmly in the soaked glove that she held proudly up.

At the crack of the bat, Jack had thrown off his mask in the catcher's reflex action to sound. Now he stood a few feet in front of home plate, refusing to look behind him as Sanchez high-fived Jones.

"Bull!" he shouted a moment later, flinging his helmet into the dugout wall after Capuccio had grounded out. "I *never* should have called that last hook!"

"You did the right thing." Marty watched the field. "He hit your guy's best pitch. I called it too. Don't worry about it."

The Sox had men on first and second when Jack came up. Eyebrows Thornton glared in, then threw a fastball that Jack smashed foul down the left-field line, spearing the box seats and scattering patrons like pigeons.

"Sit on the curve," muttered Marty. "He won't try heat again, not after that shot."

Though Eyebrows disguised it with a huge motion, the pitch was indeed a roundhouse curve, but Jack was too eager. Expecting a fastball, he overswung and struck out.

"How about the one I cranked, Pops?" the kid asked as he returned to the dugout.

Marty blew a bubble. "You should never have bit on the floater."

Jack gulped down a mouthful of water, then flattened his paper cup and slammed it against the dirt.

"He threw *you* heat on a two-two in the Stadium last week!"

Marty glared at the rookie. All he could see was youth: a face smooth and tanned, with neither crows' feet nor dark circles marring the eyes. Not washed up at thirty-two.

"I'm not you, you dummy!" Marty yelled. "I can't catch his smoke, so he can blow it by me. But *you* can, so he's gotta throw you the junk!" Because you're young and strong and your life is a dream coming true all around you, not a memory that everyone is forgetting. "You dope!" Marty cried angrily. "You dumb dope! You—"

Jack glared back, his expression torn between indignation and fear.

Don't blame him, Marty instructed himself. It's not his fault. "You've got to *think*, Jack," he said more calmly. "Use your head."

Stan Antonelli, who replaced Diego for the top of the eighth, got into immediate trouble, loading the bases with one out. Facing Harshman, a dangerous but impetuous hitter, Antonelli got skittish, backing off the pitching rubber after each delivery and rubbing the ball as if doing so could shrink its chances of being hit. After an agonizing sequence of pitches and delays, Antonelli ran the count full.

The entire stadium was on its feet, the crowd roaring, as Antonelli consulted the heavens. Jack squatted and gave the signs, but the nervous pitcher shook him off.

Something in the Yankee dugout caught Marty's eye. Reuben Pye, the pinstripes' manager, was rocking on his heels, running his fingers against the dugout wall and looking at his third-base coach.

Suicide squeeze.

The words exploded in Marty's head as if a neon sign were burning out. He darted a look to Lefty Durrell, their third-base coach, and the bright light flashed again.

They've got the bunt on!

Before he knew it, Marty had leapt to his feet, shouting "Kid!"

Jack looked impassively over.

Pitchout, signaled Marty in the private code he had patiently taught the rookie, trying to avoid attracting the Yankees' attention. His knees screamed with pain, but he held still. If the Yankees knew the Red Sox were on to them, they'd take the squeeze off.

Jack's expression was unreadable behind his crimson mask. With a tiny shrug, he squatted and signed.

The shock on Stan Antonelli's long plastic face was palpable. He looked in again, not so much shaking off the sign as refusing to believe it.

Marty cracked his knuckles. You've got to get them to trust you with their lives, he thought. Believe him, Stan!

Tugging his cap, Antonelli nodded, very slowly, then went into his motion.

It happened in an eyeblink. As Antonelli delivered, Joe Bob Hubbard broke for home and Harshman lunged for the ball. Thrown high and outside, it zipped past his shortened reach. "Strike three!" called the ump as Jack grabbed it, blocking the plate as the runner lowered his shoulder and crashed into the Red Sox catcher.

Their spectacular collision shook the entire stadium. Bodies rebounded dizzily, then fell over. Hubbard's helmet spiraled like shrapnel. Dust kicked everywhere, the umpire peering through it. Yankee and Red Sox fans alike were hushed, mesmerized by the confrontation.

To get a better view, Marty leapt up the dugout steps. His knee buckled with a pain as fresh as the shock he'd felt at age seven, and he gasped. His leg twisting, he fell against the concrete, his knee a spearing fire. It dulled into an ache that throbbed in time with his heartbeat.

Be all right, he thought at Jack.

The young catcher was sprawled on the ground, dazed. But when he raised his glove high above his head, white showed in the pocket. Slowly but steadily he stood up, collected his equipment, and trotted uninjured off the field.

In the Red Sox dugout, Marty smiled softly. He straightened up, rubbing his knee. "Good job, kid."

—·—

The Yankees still clung precariously to a one-run lead when the Red Sox came up for the bottom of the ninth.

The scoreboard changed and the crowd rustled. California had won. The pennant would be decided in Boston.

Jack led off with a walk. Eyebrows Thornton, who

had overpowered Skeeter Henry all day, threw a strike past, but on the pitch, Jack stole second.

That finished Thornton; Reuben Pye made his slow way to the mound like a bashful bill collector, and brought in Ike Williams, the Yankees' ace reliever.

"Warden, you're hitting for Ranshaker," shouted O'Connor as soon as Williams had completed his warmups. "I'll get you in this game yet," he added to Marty. "I'm having Henry bunt Lyons over. Then you. A sac fly will get us into extra innings. A homer will win it. Give 'em hell, Warden. Those New Yorkers deserve it. Let's send them Yankees into the open league with a loss, right?"

A home run's too much to expect, thought Marty, making the silent, invisible walk to the on-deck circle. Just one good at-bat. Go out the right way.

The late-afternoon sunlight was slanting over the leftfield stands, covering the diamond in shadow but bathing the bleachers in orange. He paused, taking it all in.

Swinging the weighted warmup bat to loosen his shoulders, Marty took his practice stance, his knees and legs free of soreness as he watched Ike Williams and Skeeter Henry in front of him.

Extra innings, prayed Marty. Let time stop. Let us tie them, so we can play forever and ever. Wouldn't that be a miracle?

The pitch was a curve. Henry dragged it expertly down the first-base line, the ball rolling, rolling, until for an instant it rolled foul and Ray Jones swiped it away.

Down gingerly on one sore knee, leaning on his

bat, Marty glanced into the Sox dugout. As Henry stepped out of the box, Marty read the signs Royal O'Connor gave his third-base coach.

He's taking the bunt off, Marty realized with a combination of admiration and horror. Royal, you fox! You're trying to win the game right here!

The stands were simmering with anticipatory noise, the crowd on its feet. Ike Williams rubbed the baseball and stared in to centerfield, then turned, resettled his cap, and leaned in for the sign. Marty caught his breath, as hypnotized by the moment as any fan.

On Williams's rising fastball, Skeeter lofted a high, lazy fly to left.

Oh, no, Marty thought, his stomach torn between exultation and despair. The wind's blowing it out—

In any other park in the league, Henry's flyball would have been a routine out. This was Fenway, with its famous short leftfield wall, and a strong wind. The ball whiffled in its flight—Marty could hear it clearly—staying up an impossibly long time. Then it settled like a feather into the screen for a game-winning two-run homer.

Bedlam.

Ike Williams and Marty both watched in shock as Jack scored the tying run, followed only a few seconds later by a flabbergasted Skeeter Henry, who jumped on home plate with both feet. The Red Sox poured out of their dugout, mobbing their little hero.

Fans leapt onto the field, splashing through the puddles in crazy exuberant circles. Crestfallen Yankee players shoved people aside like sandbags as they fought toward their dugout. Teenagers tore chunks of grass from the field, clustering like excited bees around the bases, trying to uproot them. Cans popped and sprayed foam on players and fans alike.

"Great game, Pops!" shouted Jack in his ear, playfully wrestling the older man along the corridor. "Heckuva call on that pitchout! You're a genius!"

Inside the clubhouse, reporters swarmed around the Boston players as they struggled in one by one, laughing and leaning on each other. A knot formed around Jack. Microphones pushed at him like autograph pencils.

As the compliments rained down on his young friend, Marty smiled, knowing how wonderful it was to have nothing ahead of you but your dreams.

"Atta boy, Jack," he said.

He undressed slowly, his knees throbbing but not painful. Betty Simmons couldn't go to the Series—she was ineligible because she had been called up after the rosters expanded. For that matter, it dawned on him without sadness, neither could Marty Warden.

When Marty dropped his uniform pants, Lizbeth's photograph fell from the back pocket. Marty grabbed for it, but the picture of his homer fluttered beyond his fingers, landing in a puddle of champagne. It curled and discolored, the images blurring.

Lizbeth has the negatives, he told himself. She can always make another. He continued undressing, watching the crumpled paper on the floor.

Now completely naked, he stared at his locker, methodically cutting through the adhesive tape and peeling away the bandages like a snake shedding its skin. His knees ached and he sat there a long time, while the sounds faded as the players and journalists trickled out.

"Pops?"

Marty looked up. Jack stood before him, fresh from his shower, the blond hair tousled. "You're retiring, aren't you?" the young man asked.

"You're not supposed to know," said Marty.

"Won't be the same without you, Pops." He held out his hand.

Marty looked at his legs, water dripping around his feet. It's over, he thought. It's finally over.

"Yeah," he said raggedly. Then he smiled, because the pain inside him was gone, and took Jack's hand. "Give 'em hell, kid."

10

FREE DAY

Peg Kerr

Liza awoke at the sixth hour as usual. For a fleeting instant, she thought that she had missed her wake-up call. Then she remembered: this was her free day, and she didn't have to get up with the other workers. Pulling the thin blanket to her chin, she drew her knees up to hoard her warmth and closed her eyes, but the habit of rising early was deeply ingrained, and sleep eluded her. Eventually, she gave up and simply lay in a pleasant half doze, listening to the early-morning stir in the barracks.

Someone gave her foot a poke. Yawning, she turned over to face Ruthann, the dark, stooped woman with the finely etched face who slept on the tier below her.

"Get a move on it, McGillus. First shift starts soon."

"Stow it. This is my free day, and I'm not leaving this bunk until I'm good and ready—or at least until someone from night shift kicks me off."

"Free day?" Ruthann's face lit up. "Sorry, I forgot."

"That's okay, I was awake." She stretched and yawned again. "What the hell, I might as well get up."

"What are you planning on doing?"

Liza sat up and reached for her battered khaki coveralls on the hook beside her bunk. "The same as usual."

Ruthann snorted derisively as she began plaiting her long, scraggly hair. "I don't know why you bother with her. With only one free day every two weeks, I'd think you'd spend it doing something sensible. Like sleeping."

Liza grinned, unoffended. She wriggled into her coveralls and dropped lightly to the floor. Folding her blanket, she tossed it up to the foot of her bunk.

Munitions barracks 52C housed twenty-four women and girls during each shift, but most of the morning shift had left for the cafeteria already, and the night shift had not yet arrived, which meant that the lineup for the washstand was gratifyingly short. Liza had been working on the munitions line for six years, starting at the age of twelve, and she had become accustomed to the grease that always covered her after every shift. Indeed, she had almost come to consider it a sort of auxiliary skin. Nevertheless, she washed now, scrubbing vigorously to make up for the lack of soap. Peering into the cracked mirror, she finger-combed her unruly auburn hair. She reached into the small footlocker at the foot of her bunk that held her few personal possessions and removed a knife, which she slid into a large open pouch at her hip. With a final wave to Ruthann, she slipped into her shoes and headed out the door for breakfast.

Breakfast was coffee and, much to her disgust, gruel. Liza considered skipping the meal, but, realizing that the old woman wouldn't have much to spare, she choked down the unappetizing mush. She lingered over a second and third cup of coffee, leaving finally when the kitchen workers began cleaning tables around her in preparation for the next meal.

At the supply room she stopped to pick up a large can of gasoline. The commissary clerk weighed out twenty pounds of dried food and boxed it for her. Positioning the box under the arm that held the can, she double-checked to make sure that she had her knife, then signed out at the front gates. After the heavy barrier swung shut behind her, she began walking quickly, occasionally readjusting the box on her hip, always keeping her free hand near the hilt of the weapon concealed in her clothing.

The streets through which she walked had once been lined with stately, venerable towers and buildings, rising so high above the pavement that they had plunged the city into a sort of perpetual twilight. The bombings had destroyed most of them, however, allowing Liza an unobstructed view of the bleak winter sun rising above the rubble. No one else was around. Although she was alert for danger, the ruins themselves did not particularly bother her. She could not remember the city any other way.

Shivering, she picked her way through the stone debris covering an empty public square and hurried past a fountain where a headless statue gestured to the skeletal remains of office buildings and apartments. A scuffling sound made her jump at one point, but it was only a few rats, scurrying away ahead of her into the shadows. She took a deep breath and walked on. At the far end of the square stood two buildings that had lost only their top two or three floors. Liza turned down the street between them. At the fifth doorway she stopped. Skirting the broken planking at the threshold, she mounted the rickety stairs, carefully stepping over the missing twelfth step.

The landing and the hallway were unlit. Cautiously, Liza groped her way along the wall until she located the door she wanted. She knocked, waited a few moments, and then knocked again, calling "It's Liza; open the door."

The door rattled as bolts were pulled back on the other side and then opened partway on a safety chain, revealing a wizened, birdlike face framed with white hair, peering out into the dim corridor.

"It's me, Mary," Liza repeated patiently. "Let me come in."

The old woman stared at Liza for a moment or two. Then, slowly, her face lit up, and a trembling hand reached, fumbling, to unhook the safety chain and open the door all the way.

"Elizabeth—Elizabeth, you came back to see me!"

Liza stepped forward into the small room.

The light from the single window did little to brighten the old woman's home. The furnishings were spartan: a small cot in the corner covered with a worn handmade spread, a bookcase with a modest, well-thumbed collection, and a wooden table and chair in the center of the room. An ancient gasoline-powered electric generator stood in another corner, with an exhaust pipe running from it, leading outside through a hole in the wall. Across the room from the bed, the shelves above the sink were graced with a few plates and bowls and two delicate porcelain teacups and saucers.

The old woman reached out to touch Liza's arm, as if to convince herself that she was really there, while the scant, difficult tears of old age started up in her eyes.

"You know that I always come back, Mary," Liza said. Gently disengaging the gnarled hand from her sleeve, she drew it down to touch the box she carried. "See what I brought you? Here, take it and have a look."

Hastily drying her eyes, the old woman took the box over to the table in the middle of the room and began struggling with the string and wrapping paper on the small parcels it contained. After closing the door and shooting the bolts, Liza took the gasoline can over to the generator and emptied it into the tank. Then she pulled the single wooden chair up to the table and sat down, grinning at Mary's delight.

The old woman muttered to herself as she examined her treasures. "Macaroni, egg powder, rice, oatmeal, cornmeal, soybeans, salt, prunes, bulgur, tea—oh, Elizabeth, onions! And dried apples, and even some sugar! And what's this?" She picked up a can and took it over to the window. Squinting at the label, she exclaimed in delight, "Canned tomatoes!"

Liza laughed. Scooping up the small packages and cans, she began arranging them on the shelf above the cracked porcelain sink. "I brought some other canned vegetables, and here's some dried milk too, Mary. Give me a kettle to boil some water, and we'll mix up a liter or so." With mock severity, she eyed the old woman who had come over to place her precious tomatoes with the rest of the loot. "You *have* been boiling the water before using it, haven't you?"

Wide-eyed, Mary stared at her in confusion. "Boil water?" She paused, thinking. "Oh, yes, I boil the water—sometimes," she added meekly as an afterthought.

Liza sighed and launched into the familiar lecture. "You *must* boil the water before using it, Mary, to kill the germs. I don't want you to get sick." She patted the frail shoulder as she filled a kettle with water and placed it on the hot plate. She flipped the switch on the generator to start it up and reached for the glass liter bottle on the shelf.

"Now tell me," she said brightly, raising her voice to speak above the rumble of the machine in the corner as she began rinsing off the bottle, "how have you been since I saw you last? Have you had any problems? Do you have anything that needs fixing?"

The old woman shuffled slowly over to the chair and seated herself with exaggerated care. "There was a man—"

"A man?" Liza turned around in alarm. "You have been keeping the door bolted, haven't you?"

"Oh, yes. He knocked on all the doors in the hallway and called. He wanted food, I think. I did not say anything, and he went away. He hasn't come back."

Mollified, Liza turned back to the sink. "That's

good. Now remember, you mustn't open the door to anyone but me, understand?"

Mary gravely nodded her head. "I will not open the door to anyone but you," she repeated obediently, and added, "I will boil the water, too."

Liza laughed as she shook the water from her hands and dried them on her coveralls. "You do that."

"The gasoline that you brought me last time has lasted long enough, but the light is broken," Mary continued. "I have no candles, so I must go to sleep early. The days in winter are so short." She sighed and added hopefully, "You can fix it, maybe?"

Liza looked up doubtfully at the naked bulb hanging from the ceiling by a cord that was connected to the generator. "I can try." She turned off the generator, pulled the table underneath the bulb, and gingerly climbed on top. The bulb didn't rattle when she shook it, so she raised herself on tiptoe to examine the cord. One short frayed section of wire had worked its way free from the cloth insulation. "It's the connection, I think."

The old woman nodded uncomprehendingly.

Liza stepped down from the table and from underneath the cot in the corner retrieved the kit of tools she had "borrowed" from the factory. There was a small coil of electrician's tape underneath the pliers. She tore off a piece, then stepped back onto the table and wrapped the tape around the cord, patching the frayed ends together.

"Try the switch."

Mary walked slowly over to the corner and flipped the switch on the generator. The bulb glowed to life, and Liza nodded in satisfaction as she descended to the floor again. The old woman beamed.

After a while, the water began to boil. Liza carefully scalded the milk bottle. She filled it again with hot water, then covered it and opened the window to place it on the narrow sill. "When it's cool, we can add the dry milk."

"Will it take very long for it to cool down?" Mary asked.

"It might take a while."

"Well, then, we can go to the park while we wait," the old woman suggested hopefully.

Liza sighed. "Mary, it's cold outside, too cold for your old bones."

"My coat is very warm. I have gloves too, and you can wear my sweater. Please, Elizabeth," she begged, "I haven't been outside since the last time that you came."

Liza shook her head. "It's not just the cold; it's dangerous out there."

Bowing her head, Mary turned away and began brushing imaginary crumbs off the table. She said nothing more, but Liza could tell by the sag of her shoulders how disappointed she was.

Liza ran her fingers through her hair in frustration and finally threw up her hands in defeat. "All right, Mary. Get your coat."

The old woman turned around again, her smile returned. "Oh, thank you, Elizabeth!" She took off the sweater she wore to give it to Liza and fetched her outer wrappings from a hook by the door. "You will see," she continued happily. "You'll be glad we went out. We can watch the children playing in the park and feed the pigeons. Maybe they will be selling hot chestnuts there too." Kneeling down carefully by the bed, she pulled out a dusty hatbox from underneath, then took it over to the table. "We can go window shopping—of course, all the Christmas decorations will be taken down by now, but there still might be some January sales. It's still January, isn't it?"

Wordlessly Liza nodded.

"Good, good!" Mary carefully wrapped a muffler over her head and around her throat. She drew from the box an Easter bonnet that had seen its first days of pristine glory perhaps twenty or thirty years ago. The drooping artificial flowers were yellowing, and quite a few cherries were missing. Reverently she placed it over the muffler and tied it firmly in place.

Liza slowly picked up the sweater that Mary had draped over the back of the chair and shrugged herself into it. She buttoned the old woman's coat for her. Then catching her elbow, she said earnestly, "Mary, I want you to be prepared when you go out there. Things have changed. The city has been ruined for years; don't you remember the bombings? Are you sure that you really want to go outside?"

"Elizabeth." The old woman took her hand and gently squeezed it. "You are the one who doesn't remember."

After Liza had turned off the generator and locked the door, they went down the stairs in silence, Liza carefully guiding Mary over the missing step. Outside, they both blinked and shaded their eyes from the sun's cold light. Mary clung to Liza's arm and looked around in bewilderment as they slowly made their way over the broken sections of pavement. Their feet crunched shards of glass fallen out of a vacated storefront's shattered windows. The faded remains of a torn awning flapped in the wind above the store's boarded-up doorway. The old woman stared at the shop sign as they passed, but the letters had been erased long ago by fire and rain.

They were forced to detour around a telephone pole that had been sheared off at its base and lay across the street. The wind whipped up swirls of dust and cinders that spun around them like phantom skaters, then disappeared.

Then they turned the corner, and Liza led the way to the forlorn city square. At the abandoned empty fountain they sat on a large stone that had been blasted from a column from the building above. The gutted frameworks of skyscrapers loomed overhead, watching them. For a long time they sat listening to the sighing sound the wind made blowing through the broken stones and girders.

Mary drew her coat closer to her throat. "It was beautiful once, Elizabeth. You can't really tell now, but that fountain was supposed to be a girl pouring water from a pitcher into a basin. I remember the flowers that were planted around it in the summer—all pink and yellow and red. And there were benches along here where people would sit and feed the sparrows and pigeons. I used to love to come here in the summer and listen to the concerts that the symphony orchestra gave at sunset. Everyone would bring picnic baskets and sit on blankets, listening to the music under the sky. The music would make you feel things . . ."

"Like what?"

"Oh, maybe happy. Or peaceful. Or it would make you imagine things. I remember one night when I was listening to the orchestra while I was looking at the sky, and I was getting a little sleepy, and suddenly it seemed to me that the music I heard was the stars singing to each other."

The two women were silent for a moment. Then Liza asked, "What else did people do in the park?"

"Well, parents used to bring their children here. Usually the children would just play with each other, but sometimes their parents would join in too."

"What would they do?"

"They might play a ball game, the whole family, or maybe fly a kite if there was enough wind."

"A kite?"

"You make it with paper and sticks of wood. It would have a string tied onto it, and you would run with it into the wind until it went high up into the air." Mary chuckled quietly to herself as Liza absorbed this. "I was never very good at flying kites. Mine always got caught in trees." She shook her head. "I remember how the children loved the puppet shows that were put on every weekend," she went on more slowly, "and how all the young couples would go walking up and down among the flower beds."

As Mary continued to speak slowly, Liza tried to imagine what the park had looked like then. But try as she might, the desolation of the abandoned square kept her imagination from seeing the pictures the old woman painted with her words. Her hands ached from the cold, and her throat ached from the loss of something that she had never known.

The old woman fell silent. They sat together in a cold reverie, listening to the restless keen of the wind.

A sudden snarl jolted Liza to her feet. She whirled around to face a large dog, which had silently approached them from Liza's side, slinking around the base of the fountain. Liza's hand crept down slowly and drew her knife. "Mary, stay back."

The broken blocks did not give her much room to maneuver. She crab-stepped to the side, hoping to lure the dog after her so that the largest stones would be between it and Mary.

The dog followed, its growl rising in crescendo. It came to a sudden stop several meters from its first position, then dog and woman studied each other. Liza tightened her grip on the hilt of her weapon, feinted with her blade, and shouted.

Hackles bristling, the dog crouched lower and then sprang for her leg. Liza dodged, whirling her arm underneath the fangs, and drew a bloody furrow along the animal's side. The dog rolled over and started for her again as she spun to face it, but the momentum and the uneven surface made her lose her balance. As she fell, the dog launched itself at her throat. She threw up her free arm barely in time to protect her jugular vein, screaming as the teeth sank in.

Desperately she stabbed at the animal's hindquarters as she struggled to shake it off. The dog lost its grip on her arm, and she managed to stab it again, this time in the flank. It yelped and, staggering to its feet, attempted to escape. Lunging, Liza delivered another blow; the dog sank to the ground, kicked convulsively, and then was still.

Liza rocked back and forth on her knees and fought to still the trembling throughout her body. She closed her eyes and heaved deep breaths, waiting for the rush of adrenaline to subside. After a while, her heart slowed down, and she opened her eyes and looked at Mary, who was staring at the dog's carcass, her eyes wide with fear.

Liza wiped her blade as clean as she could on a tuft of dead grass that had grown through the pavement and slid the knife back into her pocket. Then she got shakily to her feet and, going over to Mary's side, gently took her hand. Startled, Mary turned and stared wildly into Liza's eyes. Liza reached out and stroked her cheek slowly, wordlessly trying to reassure her. When she saw the eyes beginning to focus on her, Liza gave the frail hand a squeeze. "Come. Let's go home."

Slipping an arm around her waist, Liza helped Mary to her feet. They began walking slowly, the old woman clinging to the younger one's arm with an unexpected strength. Only after they had left the outer limits of the square did her grip begin to relax. She looked up at Liza, who smiled at her encouragingly and said, "It's all right. That dog can't hurt us now. We'll be back inside soon."

"Elizabeth," Mary whispered. "Elizabeth, that dog bit you, didn't it?"

"I'm all right. Your sweater is thick and my coveralls are tough. I'll just stop at the infirmary when I get back, and they'll give me some salve and bandage it a bit. I'll be just fine."

"Are you sure?"

"Of course I am," said Liza stoutly. "I'll tell you what—when we get back inside, I'll take a look at it. We'll mix up that milk for you and make a nice dinner—and I can curl your hair. Would you like that?"

"Oh, yes!" Mary's face finally broke into a smile, and Liza smiled back.

The wind was picking up, and they pressed on more quickly, anxious to get back indoors to warm themselves. Mary's gaze was still abstracted, and Liza, noticing, began a story to distract her.

"Do you remember me telling you about that new worker who started on the line opposite from me? Well, she got into trouble with the supervisor this week." She grinned. "You should have heard the fireworks!"

"Why, what happened?"

"Well, this new woman was having some kind of disagreement with the welder in her section, because she said the welder kept taking her tools . . ."

As Liza led Mary along, she continued to talk, including droll imitations of the other workers in her stories. By the time they had entered the apartment again, they were ruddy-cheeked from the cold and breathless from laughter.

Liza shot the bolts on the door. As Mary took her coat off and put her hat away, Liza eased the sweater off and examined her arm. The coverall cloth had ripped underneath, and her skin was already a bruised purple, but the bite marks didn't look especially deep. She rinsed her arm off over the sink with the leftover boiled water from the kettle.

"Now let's mix that milk and start dinner. We can curl your hair while we're waiting for it to cook."

She started the generator, filled the kettle and put it on to heat, placing the curling iron next to it on the hot plate. She took the cooled bottle of water off the windowsill and, after adding the dried milk powder, carefully capped it and shook it. Taking some of the packages down from the shelf, she mixed together soybeans, bulgur, and dried onions in a saucepan. When the kettle was boiling, she added some of the water to the mixture and put it on the hot plate to simmer.

Motioning Mary to a chair, Liza carefully combed out her thin short hair. Cautiously, she wrapped a rag around the handle of the curling iron.

"Hold still, now, and we'll get you all prettied up." She wrapped the sections of hair around the iron, waited, and then unwrapped them, leaving the curls, much to Mary's delight. "You look just fine!" She fetched a small mirror and held it up so that Mary could see herself.

By the time Liza finished, dinner was cooked. She dished out a helping for each of them as Mary set the spoons on the table. Then Liza pulled the bed over to the table for a seat.

The bulgur stew was hot and filling.

"I can't believe what a difference the onions make," Mary exclaimed.

"I should be jealous of you," Liza teased. "We don't get luxuries like onions very often at the factory."

They ate slowly, finishing all of the stew.

After the meal Liza brewed some of the precious tea while Mary took the two teacups down from their place of honor and wiped them off carefully.

"With sugar and milk, this is a real tea party," Mary said. She sat down on the chair again, and after turning the generator off, Liza sat back down on the bed, perching the saucer carefully on her knee. "These cups belonged to my mother," Mary said proudly. "They are almost a hundred years old." Her eyes twinkled over the brim of the cup. "Imagine—something in this room is older than me!"

Liza laughed. They sipped the tea, savoring its delicate bitterness. Then Liza leaned back and drew her legs up underneath her like a cat, allowing a delicious peacefulness to envelop her.

They sat together quietly for a long while in the darkening room. Finally Mary spoke.

"I can remember when you were just a tiny little girl. And here you are, all grown up, a good strong woman who takes care of me."

Liza opened her eyes and smiled at her.

Mary smiled back. "I was wondering, Elizabeth, whether you would like to have my teacups."

Startled, Liza exclaimed, "But, Mary, you love them so! It's not that I don't admire them, but—are you sure that you want to give them to me?"

Mary regarded her silently, and suddenly Liza understood. The old woman was dying. She wanted to show her gratitude to Liza while she still could, giving her a tangible piece of the past that she had tried to help Liza understand for so long.

Liza felt the long-forgotten prickle of tears in the corners of her eyes. Carefully, she set down the cup and saucer and leaned forward. "I'd be proud to accept your gift. But why don't we leave them here? They would be safer here than at the factory. You can enjoy seeing them on your shelf, and I can look forward to drinking out of them when I come to visit. How would that be?"

The old woman's eyes shone in the darkness. "That would be wonderful. Thank you, Elizabeth."

Reluctantly, Liza stood up and picked up the empty gas can. "I must go now, Mary. It's getting dark outside."

Mary stood up, too, and walked with Liza to the door.

"You'll come back, won't you, Elizabeth? You'll come back and see me?"

Liza nodded and enfolded the old woman in her arms. "I'll come back to see you, Grandma, next free day. You can count on me."

11

BEGGARMAN

Susan Shwartz

"And see the wounded world healed in my dreams . . ."

One more line, and he'd have the poem finished. Earth bobbed in the viewport—or maybe he bobbed in zero G; it was hard to tell—fragile and bright like the enormous soap bubbles you could blow in zero G if you weren't worrying about antisocial behavior.

Oh, this was going to be one good poem—maybe the best he'd ever written! He could just hear it . . .

"The wounded world, he says. The wooouunnded wor-ulld! Jommy, you're such a throwback!"

Jolted from his thoughts, Jommy started, bouncing at least a meter in the Rim's zero G as Andrew and Mira snatched at his poems, gracefully, careful to conserve motion. Just his luck. The most popular kids on the Habitat would have to be the ones who'd nicknamed him "Throwback." Just because he liked poems and Earth and even ate the "clone cutlets" that the Spaceborn gang hated because they were meat, and meat-eating was a filthy Earther habit.

"The wounded world!" Others of the Spaceborn surrounded him, chanting the line he had thought was so wonderful mockingly through their noses.

The new poem was ruined now, and Mira was snatching at the others.

"Waste paper, everyone! Throwback doesn't even recycle!"

"Beggarman, beggarman!"

Jommy tried to protect his poems; but low and zero G were the Spaceborns' particular habitats, not his. It made him dizzy if he moved too fast. They were taller than he, sinewy and taller as if freedom from constant one G let them stretch. Earth, and his shattered vision of it, watched as they danced about him.

Mira spooked him with a sudden shriek that'd get her downchecks if any teachers heard it and tore three leaves from his notebook. Then she gave him a shove that sent him flying so fast, his head spun and lunch threatened to heave itself back up.

He swallowed and tried to aim himself, use the inertia of his weightless body to crash into at least one of them and bump him into the frosty Rim bulkhead. The Spaceborn laughed and evaded him, kicking out at the last moment to send him flying in another direction. Unlike the time he'd told Andrew that his synthesizer music reminded him of spoiled tofu, this time they'd show no telltale bloodstains. Just clumsy Jommy, tripping over his own hands . . . and feet . . . and head. . . .

"Listen to what else old Throwback says," Andrew

shouted, beginning to read the poem—*his* private Earth dreams!—in an affectedly dramatic voice.

"That's so sick!" cried Mira. "He wants to live on a *dirtball*!"

The Spaceborn laughed and gasped at Mira's last word, which was about the worst thing anyone could say. If her parents heard her, they'd . . . they'd *talk* at her, and they were all psychs. Personally, Jommy would rather be hit. Then someone's knee caught the side of his head, and he bounced out of the sphere of jeering Spaceborn, clutching his torn papers as he caromed toward the cylinder that pierced every ring of the Habitat. Little globes of sweat flew from his forehead. The Spaceborn dodged them, shrieking with laughter.

Three Spaceborn leapt, meeting midway between deck and bulkhead to snicker and trade *dirt* stories.

"I heard there's an *Earther* here now. Came up here because he caught some sort of dirtball dis*ease* . . ."

"Earthers get all kinds of new diseases on Earth since they wiped out its ozone layer and turned the oceans to green slime . . ."

"Oh, *dirtballs*, that's *awful*!"

"Maybe he came up here to be with the Beggarman?"

"Or maybe to play with the Throwback."

"How 'bout it, Jommy, wanna meet the Beggarman?"

Could you die of shame? Jommy thought he was about to find out.

SERVICE ACCESS. He saw the words stenciled in

black across a hatch twice before they made sense. Next to them was a button and, best of all, a handle, welded onto the bulkhead beside the hatch. If he could hit the button, catch the handle as he passed, and hold on while he swung round, he might escape the capering, screaming kids.

There it was, coming up.

And then he had it! The metal burned his hand as inertia tested his grip; but he hung on, then levered himself into the crawl space and watched the square of light vanish as the hatch slid shut. He saw Mira's face, scared and so pale that she looked like she was going to throw up. In zero G too. Serve them all right if she did.

He shut his eyes, squeezing them till ugly lights exploded behind his eyelids. Once the colors made him good and sick, he let his eyes open, and blinked once.

Lights the color of Luna had come on in the crawl space, each smaller than a storage disk and not so bright.

Now, where was he? Up or down? He remembered his mother's words: "Up and down are misnomers in zero G." You didn't have altitude, just attitude. Direction, he had better call it for now. What direction did he want to go in?

He wanted to go "down," toward heavier G, maybe toward the Habitat's core where he'd be his Earthside weight. The Spaceborns hated full G, so he spent whatever time he could there. He couldn't drop; there would have to be some sort of rungs.

And there they were, gleaming in the pale glow of

the emergency lights. They made his skin look bleached out, except for the smears of dust and—was that blood or ink on one arm?

Why, he was actually dirty!

Dirty, bloody, driven away by the very people who ought to be his friends: what was wrong with him? Little spherical tears floated from his eyes and wet his hand. He rubbed them, leaving a clean streak. If he didn't move soon, the Spaceborn would probably call Security. And somehow, it would all be made his fault: Jommy the throwback, the dirtball—though they wouldn't use the word—going off by himself and writing poems. Jommy who couldn't take a joke or share when his classmates asked him to.

The time Andrew had given him a bloody nose, he'd raised such a howl of "Jommy's gone Beggarman" that the psychs had called them all in for family conference; and, no, his mother couldn't plead duty on the radiotelescope, and his father couldn't log in on the LAN.

"No one's been violent in our family since Breakaway," his mother had said. "And this Andrew, who you say is so well adjusted, accuses him of going Beggarman . . ."

"Interesting phrase," Jommy's father murmured. "Before Breakaway, I'll bet you that word was *'boogeyman.'* "

The psych glared, but not as hard as Jommy's mother. She cleared her throat.

"How will this affect Jommy's application to McAuliffe?" Dutifully his father looked up from his hand-held microcomputer and asked the proper, necessary question.

It wasn't my *fault*! Jommy had wanted to howl. But his nose had throbbed, and besides, it was useless. The psych would believe Andrew, just like all the teachers always did. *He* was certain to make McAuliffe, the institute on the oldest Habitat where all the brightest, luckiest kids got to go. Throwback Jommy'd better say his prayers that he wasn't left behind, to miss out on advanced training and friends from all the Habitats and get stuck on makework all his life.

"He's got another year," said the psych. "If he applies himself, I think I can certify that he'd be able to deal with the stress of going off-station."

Bobbing by the ladder, Jommy gritted his teeth at the memory. *Didn't they understand?* he asked himself, as he'd asked every night since then. He *was* trying. And he *had* to get into the institute; it was his only hope of getting out of here!

Out of here! Jommy grabbed the nearest rung and started climbing. He was still so light that it didn't matter if he missed a couple of rungs and floated for a little. Then he felt a slight tugging, all over his body. Soon he'd be getting closer to where there was actual weight.

Careful. Where there was gravity, there was direction; he could fall and really hurt himself. *Fall and go squish!* he thought. Tears dripped down his face, but he needed both hands—one crumpling his papers—for the ladder. Heavier and heavier he grew, and his breath came in gasps. His hands, hot from grasping the rungs of the ladder, began to blister.

Now the rungs curved round the central bulkhead, forming a little perch beside a bigger-than-normal emergency light, shining over a hatch marked EXIT. Jommy clambered into that perch and crouched there. What was it his father had told him? "We named you Jommy for a boy in a story. He was very special and very brave." Just last year he had come across that story in his father's collection of disks. Jommy wasn't a name for someone special and brave; it was the name of a freak people chased! He'd certainly lived up to *that*, hadn't he?

He cried for a while, till he thought of Security, chasing him through the shaft.

Fear brought him fully alert. Below the EXIT marks were codes that indicated what deck and subdivision level he had reached. Just as he thought, he was near the one-G core. *Better get out.* He pressed the red button and, when the hatch hummed aside, thrust himself out into the too-bright corridor.

His timing was like everything else in his life—rotten! Wouldn't you just know he'd hear footsteps? Heavy footsteps, the steps of an adult confident of his right to go where he pleased.

The footsteps drew nearer, but there was something strange about the way they sounded. Not *thud-thud*, or even the *pad-pad* of the surefooted Habitants; but a sort of *thud-click*, as if the someone wore metal on his feet.

The footsteps paused. Jommy knew how he must look: a dark-haired, grubby boy, clutching smeared and torn papers, crouching by an emergency hatch.

"What's this?" asked a voice he had never heard

before. It was deeper, more richly accented than the Habitants'. Jommy looked down at the intruder's boots and understood why his steps had sounded so strange. Attached to the boots were small metal plates that he knew could be magnetized in low-G areas. Only one type of person would wear such boots: someone who wasn't used to low G. Someone from Earth.

Jommy had just met the Beggarman.

Even as Jommy tried to squeeze himself into the bulkhead and disappear, the Beggarman laughed.

"Why do I get the feeling I'm supposed to say 'Fee, fie, fo, fum'?" he asked. He backed up a step or two. "Get up and run, lad, if that's what you want."

The laugh and friendly words stopped Jommy in midscramble. The Earthman didn't look like the Beggarman. The Beggarman should be skeleton-thin, dressed in rags he hadn't changed since Breakaway when he'd sneaked on board the last ship to flee Earth. He should have hungry, vacant eyes. And above all, the Beggarman would never step back to let anybody run.

What Jommy saw instead was a man in late middle age, wearing the same sort of worksuits that everyone wore. But the scars of sun and gravity were upon him. Like Jommy, he was shorter than the usual Habitant. His hair was streaked with gray. His skin was wrinkled and darker—*tanned*, the word was—and his eyes, under thick, thick eyebrows, were very bright.

"You were expecting . . . what? Some sort of monster? Instead, you met me. Sorry to disappoint you. Dr. George I. Stewart, at your service," said the

Earthman. "The I's for Isherwood; my father had a strange sense of humor. Want a hand?"

Jommy shook his head and braced himself against the wall, his free hand patting the dust from his sides and backside.

"Care to tell me your name?"

The Privacy Codes said you didn't have to give your name. You didn't even have to be nice if you thought you were in trouble. Just step out into the corridor and call the nearest Security Monitor for help. But would the real Beggarman give his name, even make a little joke out of it, then spread out his hands to show he meant no harm?

Tentatively Jommy smiled back. The man didn't look as if he were going to—what was the bad Earther word?—*mug* Jommy.

"I'm Jommy," he told the Earther at last, feeling awful even as he said it. He'd had the same feeling the first time he'd taken free-fall drill. Only that time he'd thrown up.

"Maybe you'll tell me your last name later. It couldn't be 'Cross' by any chance, could it?"

Jommy grinned. That was the name of his namesake in the book *Slan*. The Earther grinned back, an I-didn't-think-so-either sort of smile. Oh, Jommy hoped the Spaceborn were lying about Earthers.

"Well, we're both named for loners. And I'd say, young Jommy, that we're both pretty far from where we're supposed to be. If this were my home, I'd guess you'd been in quite a fight. Who won?"

Jommy let his wad of papers fall. By now Mira had probably cried all over her parents and told them some sort of awful story. He'd *never* get into the McAuliffe now; he'd be stuck here forever, a disappointment to his parents and a bad example for the little kids.

This George Stewart man stooped and picked up the paper, began to read. Flick . . . flick . . . his eyes went, like a scanner trained on computers just like they had on the Habitat. He raised an eyebrow.

"No-oo!" Jommy darted at him. It was the Spaceborn all over again, stealing and jeering at his poems.

"Steady there!" Stewart said, smoothed out the papers, and returned them. "Some of these lines are really good. I especially liked the one about the 'wounded world.' That's precisely what we're doing on Earth, you know. Healing it. Making it a garden again."

Jommy slid to a stop. "They *are*? I mean, you *are* healing Earth? I mean, you like my poems?" The questions tumbled out as untidy as his room until breathlessness made him stop. He gasped for air and indignation, finishing with "Why are you reading my stuff?"

"Were you fighting to protect them?" asked the Earthman.

"They're *private*!" Jommy said.

"And someone grabbed them. Probably started reading them to someone else. And you only wanted to crawl into a hole and pull it in after you, right?"

"That's just what I did!" Jommy admitted. "Climbed down from the Rim in a maintenance shaft."

"Did you ever come that way before?" Dr. Stewart looked genuinely impressed. "I wouldn't want to take that climb in the near dark. Not to mention the low G. It still makes me sick. Nice going."

Somehow, Jommy found himself walking alongside the Earthman, describing his escape routes. "Most of them lead to full G," he finished up. "The Spaceborn don't come down here much, but I do."

They passed a washroom. At that moment, Jommy would have traded any hope he'd ever had of the McAuliffe for a chance to go in and wash. What if this stranger followed him inside? It wouldn't be Jommy's fault, but who'd believe him?

The Earthman leaned against the bulkhead. "You look like you found every speck of dust in that whole crawlway. Go wash. I'll wait outside."

A squirt of recycled water and a chemical towel could do wonders, Jommy thought as he marched outside. He felt better now; he could be brave and well adjusted now. And then Dr. Stewart cocked his head at him and looked at him, *really* looked, the way the psychs did just before things got more uncomfortable than usual.

"I wonder," he began, and Jommy chilled. As if Dr. Stewart could actually read him like his own poems, he smiled slightly, reassuringly. "No, I'm not going to break Privacy. Believe it or not, we do learn manners on Earth. Even respect for other people's rules. About these Spaceborn—sounds like they've been on your back . . ."

Jommy looked blank.

"I mean, teasing you for quite some time. Now, I'd

be the last person to say I understood Habitant customs, but don't you have rules about harassment? Seems to me that what they're doing violates those rules."

Jommy's face flushed, and he felt himself scrunching up as if someone had tried to hit him.

"You think I'd *tell*?" he demanded in a rush of anger that left him feeling deflated, yet lighter than he'd felt in months. "You know what happens when you tell? They talk at you for hours: talk, talk, talk. You really think they'd believe *me*? The Spaceborn are the most popular kids in class. I'd just be Jommy the throwback, Jommy the freak, trying to get attention. Jommy the *squealing* freak."

"Jommy Cross wasn't a freak."

"Yeah? Then why'd he have those antennae? And what would *you* call a slan?"

"I'd call him the sort of man who helps heal his society."

Ignoring the Earther's answer, Jommy spat the words out with loathing. "Now I'll never get into the McAuliffe Institute, never get off this . . . this . . ." To his horror, his eyes were filling and his voice was shaking, so he made sure to say the worst thing he could. "This filthy *dirtball*!"

And now he was going to cry, and this Dr. Stewart would report him for maladjustment. A hand touched his arm, and Jommy tensed. "I'm not Beg . . . I mean crazy!" he protested. Every Habitant knew that outbursts of temper led to Beggarman behavior.

"Of course you're not," said Dr. Stewart. He looked as if he wanted to hug Jommy, but then he glanced up, saw the red light of the Security Monitor, and let his hand drop. "You've got a right to feel bad and let it out. There's nothing wrong with you but your choice of cursewords. 'Filthy dirtball' indeed—as if dirt were something bad. Come with me, Jommy. *I'll* show you dirt. I'll show you *real* dirt!"

He started down the corridor so rapidly that Jommy broke into a scamper to keep up. He dashed tears from his cheeks with both hands just in time to see Dr. Stewart lay his palm against a lock above which was stenciled HYDROPONICS (backup). The door slid aside with a *whoosh* and a rush of warm, fragrant air, and the Earthman led the way in.

Jommy paused at the entrance. Already sticky, he'd have paid hard money—assuming he owned any—to escape this visit to hydro. He hated hydro and the time that every kid had to put in on it. Hydro was hot; hydro was sticky; and, rather than ruin clothing that had to be recycled, you had to work bare. The Spaceborn always teased him. *"What's that pouch round Jommy's waist?" "What waist?" "Oh, that's just his stomach." "When's the baby due?"*

Still, he supposed he'd better be polite.

Now Dr. Stewart was standing by what had to be the strangest-looking hydro tank Jommy had ever seen, and he was grinning as if he dared Jommy to follow.

If he tells me it's for my own good, I'm out of here, Jommy promised himself. Instead, Dr. Stewart stuck his hand in the tank and brought it up. Jommy winced: Contaminating hydro was about as low as you could get.

But no nutrient solutions dripped from the Earthman's hand. Instead, he held out clumps of crumbling brownish-black stuff, which he allowed to rain back into the tank.

"What's *that*?" Jommy asked.

"*That*, my boy, is *earth*. Honest-to-goodness, brought-from-the-homeworld *dirt*. If you want to be polite, you can call it *soil*. It works like the hydroponics solutions. Like it?"

Jommy shook his head no, yet found himself drawn to the tub of earth. The lattices of the carrot greens were oddly dark and squat; the tomato plants huddled close to the surface of the . . . the *soil*. There were rows and rows of curiously vivid plants, all smaller than they should be, and all a bright green.

"They're so *short*!" Jommy muttered. "Not like hydro on H-deck at all."

"Those spindly mutants?" Dr. Stewart challenged him. "You let a plant grow in one-quarter G, and spindly is what you get. I've got a tank up there as a control group. Plants weren't made to shoot up like that."

Jommy knew what was right to say: Plants weren't made to be dosed with pesticide till they poisoned the very folk who ate them either.

"Come on, boy," said Dr. Stewart. Jommy noticed that the door had not yet closed and felt reassured.

He crept toward the tank and, at Dr. Stewart's nod, touched the black soil. It was moist and warm from the lights overhead. He picked it up, sniffed at it.

"That's one sort of soil. We've got loam, chalky soil, peaty soil—different soils for different parts of the world. They all smell different; all *taste* different, I've been told, though I can't bring myself to try it. And we're bringing them all back."

"Healing the ecosystem?" In his earliest lessons, Jommy had learned to revere the ecosystem and learned also how Earth had destroyed its own balance of nature.

"Don't call it an ecosystem, boy. Call it a world. A home!" Stewart's voice was so rich that Jommy realized that the man was homesick for that glowing blue world that hung in the black sky.

"This is home," Jommy said.

"This is a *habitat*," said Stewart. "One asteroid, though, and all it would be is a former habitat. One longer-than-normal solar flare, and you'd all be cowering in shelters, doing genetic testing, and worrying how many eyes your grandchildren might have. Earth, now, Earth is a home, a home world that can recover if an asteroid hits it or a solar flare strikes. As it's doing right now."

"You *like* Earth?" Jommy had wanted things without hope for too long not to recognize longing when he heard it.

"God, do I miss it."

"I wouldn't miss *here*," Jommy admitted.

The Earthman smiled. "I could tell you about Earth, if you liked. If your parents agreed."

Jommy put his hands firmly behind his back. "Why?"

"A bargain. Maybe I need help."

Jommy raised his eyebrows as he'd once seen a teacher do at a particularly obvious excuse.

"Look at this!" The Earthman pulled up a carrot and held it out to Jommy.

"You'll waste it!" Jommy yelped.

Stewart shook his head, wiped off the carrot—more brightly orange than any Jommy had ever seen, and, grinning at Jommy's shock, bit into it. Surely no vegetable ever made such a satisfying crunch.

"Want one?" Stewart asked, with his mouth full. His bad manners were reassuring, but Jommy shook his head. The idea of eating something that had grown in actual dirt made his mouth water the way it did in zero G or just before he got sick.

"Next time," Stewart muttered. "Or go on up to hydro and try one of the carrots like you're used to. Then come back and eat one of these. Test them. In fact . . ." He eyed Jommy with such obvious speculation that the boy laughed.

"Much as I like it, I'm only a part-time gardener."

What do you do? It was a breach of Privacy to ask, so Jommy didn't.

"Here's the bargain. I tell you about Earth. In return, I could use someone to help me with my plants. Measure the growth of plants at Earth G against those raised in low G. Test vitamin content, taste: that sort of thing. Keep good records, then write them up. What do you think?"

I hate hydroponics. Jommy almost blurted it out.

The Earthman was watching him with a not-quite-grin. "Not a gardener, are you?"

Jommy shrugged. What if he did tend some plants and make some notes? He knew he could write up a good report—and after the day's episode with the

Spaceborn, he knew he'd never have the nerve to read "Earth Dreams" to anyone, much less submit his poems to the McAuliffe. Besides, he could keep his coverall on, and there wouldn't be any girls around to giggle at him. And besides that, being enthusiastic about vegetables and nutrition was considered *very* well adjusted. It beat growing crystals or writing synthesizer music that made your eyeballs ache to listen to it—like some of the Spaceborn did—and it would look great on the McAuliffe application.

The next day, Jommy had begun carefully to weed plants when Dr. Stewart came in with a package.

"Do you like music?" he asked, waving an iridescent disk at the boy.

"Not like Andrew writes. It makes my eyes ache."

"Try this," the Earthman said, and fitted the disk into the player he had brought. Waterfalls of sound poured over Jommy: triumphant horns lifting above a steady current of strings and a bedrock of drums.

"That's not synthesized," Stewart told him. "Every note comes from human breath, wood, gut"—Jommy grimaced—"and human talent, not chance or programming. This is old-style music. Earth music."

The music slowed, rang out over the drumbeats. Abruptly it stopped. "Here," said Dr. Stewart, "see for yourself." He lifted the disk, pretended to toss it to Jommy, who protested with an upheld, dirty hand. *To the New World* read the label.

"Why'd I bring it?" asked the Earthman. "They say plants like music. You can test it: Dvorak on one group and computer-synthesized squawks on another."

Then he was gone. The disk shone temptingly, its light shimmering as the door slid shut. Hastily Jommy scrubbed his hands, fitted disk into player, and let the triumphant horns surge over him. It was a wonder, he thought, that the plants did not rustle in time with it.

Weeks later into what Dr. Stewart called the growing season, Jommy hurried into hydro. Quickly he turned on the tapes, then began his day's work. Counting, weighing, and measuring went rapidly, now that he was used to it. Quickly and meticulously, he entered his results in his database.

"Elegant programming, Jommy," Jommy's Comp Sci teacher told the class. He looked as surprised at what he was saying as the Spaceborn. "I imagine that your database must be really easy to use."

Jommy ducked his head. He used to struggle just to make his teachers focus on him, not get that glazed-over look in their eyes before they called on someone more prestigious.

Two or three of the Spaceborn glared at him. "He thinks he's so great," Andrew grumbled.

"Now, Andrew, you're much too well adjusted to sink to jealousy. Don't you know how it can poison your thoughts?"

Jommy tuned out on what sounded like the sort of

helpful, well-meant lecture on cooperation that had always made him squirm with humiliation.

Andrew only grimaced. With his mind on his plants and his music, Jommy was surprised how little pleasure that gave him. If Andrew was in trouble, it would probably be for the first and last time.

I'll *get* you, dirtball, Andrew mouthed, and Jommy knew he, too, was in trouble. Again. When class ended, he scuttled out, making himself small, so small he overheard his teacher talking to a friend.

"Jommy's database was a first-rate piece of work," the Comp Sci teacher said. "Tell you frankly, I didn't think that he had it in him. He's always been sort of an underachieving lump. Now it turns out he's simply a late bloomer."

The friend muttered something about the psychs and tin gods. Both teachers laughed.

"He doesn't let it go to his head," Jommy heard his teacher say.

That couldn't be the old Throwback the teacher was talking about, could it?

"You programmed this?" his father said that evening. For once Jommy hadn't had to compete with the terminal for his father's attention. Both of them were bent over it, testing Jommy's work.

"This is excellent," he approved, just as Jommy's mother walked into the main room.

"What is?" she asked.

"Program our Jommy wrote."

Our Jommy. His eyes filled with tears. His mother

bent over him, kissed his hair, then turned her eyes to the screen.

"He's better at it than I am," she said. "That's not hard. But I can still tell fine work from a kludge. Anyone mind if we order from Central Kitchen? I know it's my turn to cook, but I need to get back to the observatory. We'll need the extra credits to equip you for McAuliffe, Jommy. I won't have you in class with my old teachers looking like something that even the Beggarman would throw away."

Getting the approval he'd always wanted was great, but what Jommy mostly heard was the music of horns and strings, and Dr. Stewart's voice, telling him of Earth. His stories made what had been dry tapes on geology or ecology come alive—and his teachers' smiles became beams. The music of Earth had fully caught him now. The sound was a river, sweeping him along, occasionally tossing him into side eddies as he caromed off a bulkhead in low G.

"Slow down!" Dr. Stewart cried. The Earthman was unsteady in the low G, squeamish about entering weightlessness, which he remembered with loathing from the trip from Earth to the Habitat. Jommy was surprised how easy it was to help him. The practice he was getting in switching grav levels made him very sure, just as his time in the one-G hydro lab was making him strong. He didn't even think of laughing. Instead, throughout the trip to the Rim, whenever Dr. Stewart asked him to slow, Jommy would bound back to help him.

"I feel like a crippled old man," grumbled the Earthman. He swallowed, his face turning slightly green.

Jommy knew those signs. If Dr. Stewart was sick here, there would be a terrible mess to clean.

"Look around you," he urged. "Listen. Even now, there are people up here, playing zero-G volleyball. There's a whir—someone must be in the minimills. You know, we manufacture equipment here and send it back to Earth."

"Ball bearings, medical supplies, and semiconductors," agreed Dr. Stewart. He looked around, more curious now than sick.

Jommy sighed with relief, but continued. "We always have to keep a lookout. You know, you tell me that Earth is safe, Earth heals, that there's room for mistakes on Earth. That sounds good to me, because here we don't dare make any mistakes. Not with vacuum outside."

"Sounds risky," said Dr. Stewart, in a tone that meant "just teasing."

"So does Earth," Jommy retorted. "Still, we're all managing, aren't we?"

He knew he sounded obnoxious, like the Spaceborn, lecturing Dr. Stewart. But the man just grinned.

"Streetwise," he said, and Jommy looked puzzled. "That's a survival mechanism. Somehow, just as you said, we muddle through. And Earth abides."

Jommy looked up at him. Stewart's words sounded like Privacy subjects, but if Jommy didn't ask, he might burst.

"Earth abides?" Stewart repeated, making it a

question. "It's the truth. But it's also the name of a book. Maybe you'd like to read it one day."

Jommy could see his parents' faces. *"Where did you get this, Jommy?" "The Beggarman gave it to me."*

"We're almost at the Rim," Jommy assured him. "You're doing fine."

Jommy floated through the last pressure door, unsealing it and making certain that Stewart bobbed past before it could close, and the Earthman muttered something about role reversal. But he chuckled while he said it.

"What I do for my work," he said.

Now that was too good a chance to pass up.

"What *do* you do back . . . home?" Jommy asked. Maybe they were good enough friends now that asking wouldn't violate Privacy.

"I touch the future."

"That's the McAuliffe Institute's motto," the boy said. "Are you a teacher?"

Dr. Stewart looked thoughtful. "On Earth we're all teachers," he said. "Let me tell you a story about a wise man. He once said that all you need for a school . . . wait a second, slow down! . . . was a log and two people sitting on either end."

Jommy thought of his Habitat's learning skills center, the labs and the computers and the fiber-optics workshops, not to mention the psychs. It would be nice to sit on a log—whatever that was—with someone like Dr. Stewart and just listen.

"And you know what, Jommy? The good thing about that sort of school is that if you're really poor, you can do without the log!"

"We're almost here." Jommy waited for Dr. Stewart to finish his story. "One more lock." They bobbed in the no gravity as they neared the heavy door. With a flourish, he palmed the viewport lock. He heard a deep intake of breath and reached around for the hand-held suction pump mounted next to the oxygen on the bulkhead.

But Dr. Stewart didn't look like he was going to be sick. Instead, he held out his palm, as if to touch the gleaming, distant world. The wounded world.

"Dear Earth, I do salute thee with my hand," he murmured.

Jommy wondered at the language. It had the rhythm of music. Dr. Stewart sounded like one of the tapes of the classics that only teachers ever listened to. The Earthman blinked fast, but not before a tear floated away from his face.

Then Jommy thought he heard a rustle, the snick of a lock being released. He spun around . . .

Too fast. Inertia flung him against the bulkhead, and Dr. Stewart laughed. Jommy was surprised that it didn't hurt when Dr. Stewart laughed at him.

"What did you say about being careful?" he asked, and they both laughed again. A minute later Dr. Stewart was pointing out Earth's continents on the tiny, brilliant globe.

They didn't mention the sounds again.

Jommy swung down the corridor in one-G country toward his hydro lab. It would take him ten more steps, he guessed, to go from the lift to the door. He was growing fast. At the start of his experiments, it used to take him fifteen. He walked fast, not noticing the bleakness of the corridors. Few of the Spaceborn cared to venture down to full G, so no one decorated bulkheads that few would see and admire. Soundproofing was good down here, but even now, Jommy ought to be able to hear the music that he kept on for his plants.

They reacted well to old Earth music like Dvorak and Bach, who wrote in patterns more intricate than a computer program. But plants that had to listen to a tape of Andrew's music that Jommy'd "borrowed" from school tended to shrivel and wilt. Still, he couldn't write "thrived to Bach" and "shriveled and wilted because of synthesizer music" in his report without backing up his claims. The McAuliffe applications and references were due in a few days.

Then the music boomed, and something else—within the lab—boomed too. Jommy flattened himself against the corridor, trying to walk without sound in the full gravity, and glad that he was used to it. A crash, muffled by the drums, followed the boom.

Jommy darted for the nearest service access, flung himself through the hatch, and grunted when it proved to be a tight fit.

Time got tight too, as the hydro door *whoosh*ed open, releasing music and whispers into the corridor. Then the music died, and someone giggled. In the cleanliness of the maintenance shaft, Jommy could smell the green earth scents he had come to love.

Three of the Spaceborn—Andrew, Mira, and Chris—ran out. Or they would have run if they hadn't had to stop every few steps and moan about their aching backs and legs. They left brown footprints, as if they'd been stepping in soil.

"Oh, *no*!" Jommy whispered. He slid out of the service hatch and ran for hydro as fast as if this were shelter drill.

When he got to the door, he stopped. The place looked like a meteor had hit. Tubs were overturned, and dirt and the clear hydro solution had blended into a horrible muck. His plants lay plucked and scattered across the filthy floor. Computer's lights were on—no one would ever deliberately crash a system—but a glance across the room at it told Jommy that his database had been wiped. And the disk that had held so much music lay scratched and bent.

His experiments. His plants. His report. His music.

"Those dirtballs," Jommy said quietly.

Then the tears came, and he scrubbed at them with one dirty hand.

"Dirtballs!" he shouted.

Sense would be to call Security. Sense would be to find his teachers or his parents or Dr. Stewart. Abandoning sense, Jommy tracked the Spaceborn by their dirty footprints down the corridor to the lift.

Seeing his face, Mira backed off. Andrew tried to run, but he was slow and awkward in the one G. Chris, who had always been a sneak, stuck out a grimy boot. It caught between Jommy's feet and he went over. In the last moment before he sprawled, he wrenched his body around so he toppled into Andrew. Andrew, Chris, and Jommy crashed onto the floor, grunting, punching, and kicking, while Mira shrieked at the Security Monitor.

"Jommy's gone Beggarman," she reported, tears in her sweet, earnest voice. "Oh! Andrew's nose is bleeding. Jommy hit him."

And hit him again and again. They had destroyed his lab. They had destroyed his work. They'd made him disappoint his friend. This was *worse* than it had been months ago, before he met Dr. Stewart, because now he had hoped, he had so hoped . . .

Tears blinded his eyes, and Andrew got in a lucky punch. Jommy yelled with pain and outrage, and punched back hard.

Trankspray filled the air. Even as Jommy felt himself going limp, he borrowed a description of the mist from one of Dr. Stewart's stories: cool and sweet as a summer's evening. Everyone went suddenly quiet.

Under the influence of the spray, Jommy found himself thinking clearly. Maybe things weren't so bad. Tubs could be turned upright, plants replanted, floors scrubbed—and his data were backed up. "There are only two kinds of users," his father had always said. "Happy users, and fools who don't download."

"We just wanted to see his plants," Mira was saying in a terrified whine, "but he threw over the tubs and chased us down the corridor. We tried to get away, but he tackled Andrew and Chris!"

"What a lie," Jommy said, disgusted, through lips that felt rubbery. "They couldn't run in full G. I watched them wreck my lab . . ." To his shame, his voice broke.

"Throwback," crooned Andrew, and then Jommy knew the worst of it. No one would believe him. They would all think he had gone Beggarman.

Beggarman, Jommy thought as boots clattered down the corridor, the long, unsteady footsteps of Habitants unused to one G, the shorter, firmer strides of . . .

"Dr. Stewart!" he tried to shout. It came out a croak.

The Earthman reached Jommy about the same time as his parents.

"What happened?" Three voices asked at once.

"They wrecked the lab," Jommy said. "I bet the one at one-quarter G is smashed too."

"Why would Andrew, Chris, and Mira wreck your lab experiments?" a teacher who had never liked Jommy much asked. "You've never been especially good neighbors with them, but they're well-adjusted children; they wouldn't do something like that."

A Security woman spoke into her wristcom in an undertone. "He's right," she confirmed. "The lab in the one-quarter-G complex has been vandalized."

Jommy moaned. He'd never get into McAuliffe. Worse than that, he would probably be sent to the psychs until he was as old as Earth. To his astonishment, bloody as he was, his mother put her arms around him.

"Why didn't you tell us you weren't happy?" she asked, her face twisting like Mira's, as if she were going to cry too. "Whatever it is, Jommy. It doesn't matter. Just get well!"

I didn't do it! Jommy thought, furious. He wanted to break away from the wrangle of adults, but the trankspray made him feel as if he'd been running through two G. Maybe three.

"Wait a moment," said Dr. Stewart. No one but Jommy heard him.

"Listen to me!" boomed the Earthman, and everyone started.

"There's truth in dirt," he said. "Look at the children's boots. Now, if Jommy had overturned his own plant tubs, he'd have gotten his boots dirty. But look at his feet. He's picked up some of the dirt on the floor, but it hasn't been ground into his boot soles. Now, look at the other three. Go on, look at them!"

To Jommy's surprise, the Security officers obeyed as if they had been preschoolers.

"Rubbed in, right?" said Stewart.

The Security people nodded.

"Give me the comm," said Dr. Stewart. "Hartley?"

Could he mean Chief Counselor Hartley? Could he call her just like that? Other people had to make appointments to see her, and call her by titles, but Dr. Stewart treated her just like he treated Jommy.

Hartley's voice, known throughout the network of Habitats, replied. "What is it, Mr. Minister?"

"Can you come down to one G? We've had some sabotage," said Dr. Stewart. "Involving the people I told you about. I'd say it's important."

"On my way," said the chief counselor.

Chief Counselor Hartley arrived in full G with one hand pressed to the small of her back. She was tall, thin, and almost eight months pregnant.

"Counselor," Dr. Stewart said, ducking his head in what Jommy realized had to be an old-fashioned bow, "my sincere regrets at dragging you down here. Someone bring Counselor Hartley a chair!"

Jommy's father was the first to comply. Dr. Stewart made a little ceremony of seating the counselor. She tried to protest, but sighed with relief as she sank down.

Seeing the counselor had taken the words out of Jommy's mouth, but not for long. Just as he opened his mouth, his mother pressed his shoulder to silence him.

"*Mr. Minister?*" his mother asked, in the special tone she kept for faulty data.

"Earth's Minister of Education," said Counselor Hartley.

So his Dr. Stewart *had* been a teacher once, after all. Jommy sagged more with relief than from the trankspray; he hadn't been lied to.

Questions erupted from three sets of parents—Andrew's, Mira's, and Chris's—from Security, and very feebly, from Jommy himself.

Dr. Stewart held up a hand. "We've got a case of sabotage," he said. "This young man did a pretty professional job on some lab work for me—Jommy, do you have a backup on your data?"

Jommy nodded.

"Apparently, some of his classmates decided to break up the place a little. And Jommy—well, he caught them at it, and lost his temper."

"Lost his temper!" one of Mira's fathers shouted, though Jommy noted that he never moved from where he stood. "Went Beggarman and *hit* people."

That caused a muttering: violence, the threat of Earth-style violence, which the Habitat was built to escape from. And Jommy had revived it.

Kiss McAuliffe good-bye, he told himself. But he had known that all along.

"Counselor," said Dr. Stewart, Mr. Minister Stewart, the old trickster, "if you look at the children's shoes, you can see who was in the lab and who wasn't."

The woman nodded. "Highly antisocial," she said.

The Spaceborns' parents shrank: antisocial tendencies meant downchecks on their records and psych sessions all around.

Jommy almost grinned, but "Quiet, you!" growled Dr. Stewart. Jommy's mother's hand tightened on his shoulder.

"And what of our son?" she asked.

"I know you had plans for him. The McAuliffe, I believe?"

What else was there? You went to McAuliffe or you went nowhere all your life. McAuliffe would never take a boy who'd gone Beggarman.

His mother nodded. "But this violence!" Her hand shook for a moment, then steadied. "I don't know where he learned it, but he's our son, and we'll see him through this."

That meant the psychs and therapy. Medicines, probably, and re-education. Jommy shut his eyes and stifled a groan.

"Not precisely," said Dr. Stewart. "You may have guessed that I take an interest in the boy."

Jommy's father started forward, his face red as Jommy had never seen it.

Counselor Hartley held up a hand. "I was aware of this. When the minister arrived here, he told me he would be visiting each habitat, looking for young people who were failing to thrive . . ."

" 'A bad fit' were the words I used," put in Dr. Stewart.

"You make my son sound like he's some sort of freak." Jommy's father clenched his fists.

"I see where he gets his urge to violence," remarked Dr. Stewart. "I don't think Jommy is a freak at all. On the contrary. He's stood up well under abuse, worked hard. And he was very kind, despite a highly prejudiced upbringing"—Dr. Stewart grinned at the sensation *that* caused—"to a stranger, even to the point of mastering his dislike of zero G. My ministry is looking for boys and girls like Jommy who don't fit on their habitats, who show signs that they might adapt to Earth."

"I'm not letting my son go live on a dirtball," Jommy's mother burst out.

"What do you want him to do? Squeeze into McAuliffe and hate every minute of it? Or not go, and wind up—with his talents—doing maintenance?" Stewart snapped. "I'm offering Jommy a ride to Earth, training there, a chance to be one of the first generation of people who can live on a planet *or* in space. Oh, he'll go to the McAuliffe, all right. Later on, as an instructor, to teach the less flexible kids. To heal the angers and misunderatndings since the Breakaway. To heal the split that's grown up between planet and habitat, Earthborn and Spaceborn.

"And, if we ever, ever manage to escape this solar system, it'll be people like Jommy we'll need on the ships. I had a reason for setting him the experiment I did. You've been growing hothouse plants up here. I think we need something hardier."

Jommy sighed. It was all he could manage.

"Well, Jommy, what do you think?" Stewart spoke to him, not to the adults. "Ready to leave the greenhouse?"

"For the greenhouse effect?" The words leapt out before he could stop them, but Dr. Stewart was too important for people to scold Jommy in his presence. Suddenly Jommy yawned. Stupid trank was making him sleepy.

"We've got the greenhouse effect under control. But don't worry. We've got other problems you can sink your teeth into." Stewart grinned again, and Jommy grinned back.

Jommy's arm still itched from immunizations, but he couldn't scratch. His pressure suit was too thick, and, besides, he was strapped into his couch, waiting for the faint bump that meant that the Earth shuttle had left the Habitat, had left home. Though zero G no longer troubled him, he swallowed hard.

He was on his way to Earth!

"You'll have to work hard and justify the minister's trust," people had been lecturing him since his future had suddenly met him in a mud-tracked corridor. And Jommy had nodded gravely and fought off grins as he remembered Dr. Stewart's last comments. "First, I was the Beggarman. Now I'm Mr. Minister. You shouldn't even *talk* to the Beggarman, but it's fine, of course, if Mr. Minister gives you a going-away gift. So, here."

It wasn't a disk or a tape, but a real book with *Earth Abides* stamped in worn gold on the fraying cover.

Never mind his baggage allowance. He left out one pair of boots that would probably not be heavy enough anyway and packed Dr. Stewart's gift instead.

There came the bump. For a minute, panic gripped him. Then the shuttle turned, and an image of Earth appeared on its screens. The music of Earth, strings, horns, and drums calling him to a new world, rose in his imagination. He was going home.

12

OLD GLORY

Bruce Coville

Donald Henderson
Civic Responsibility Class

Ms. Barnan
Sept. 15, 2041

ESSAY: The Day I Did My Duty
by
Donald B. Henderson

My great-grandfather was the craziest man I ever met. Sometimes it was embarrassing even to have him be part of the family.

For example: You should have seen how he acted when Congress passed the S.O.S. law last June.

He actually *turned off* the holo set!

"Well, that's the end of life as we know it," he said

as the image started to fade. Then he stared at the floor and started to mutter.

"Oh, Arthur, don't be ridiculous," said my mother.

She switched the set back on and waited for the newsgeek to reappear in the center of the room.

"Ridiculous?" yelped Gran-Da. "You want to see ridiculous? I'll show you ridiculous!" He stood up and pointed to the big flag that hangs over our holo set. "That's ridiculous! Thirteen stripes, sixty-two stars, and not a bit of meaning. After what they did today, it's all gone."

"That's not so, Grampa," said my father quietly. His voice was low and soft, the way it gets when he's really angry. "Now sit down and be quiet."

That was a relief. After Gran-Da came to live with us, I was always afraid he was going to get us into trouble. So I felt better whenever Dad made him be quiet. Sometimes I wished Dad would just throw him out. I didn't really want him sleeping on the streets, like all the old men I walk past on the way to school. But I didn't want to make our Uncle angry either.

Later that night, when I was going to bed, Gran-Da called me into his room.

"How you doing?" he asked.

I shrugged. "I'm okay."

Gran-Da smiled. "Are you afraid of me?"

I wanted to say no. Only that would have been a lie. So I just nodded my head.

"Afraid I'll talk dangerous?"

I nodded again. I didn't know what I would do if my friends were ever around when he started talking like he does sometimes. I knew what I *should* do, of course. But I didn't know if I could do it. I mean, he *was* my great-grandfather, even if he was crazy and wicked.

He looked sad. "Are all the kids at your school like you?" he asked.

"What do you mean?"

"Scared little sheep, afraid to talk."

"I'm not afraid to talk," I said loudly. "I just don't talk nonsense, like . . ."

I broke off.

"Like me?" he asked, scratching at the little fringe of white hair that circled the back of his head. (I don't know why he never got his head fixed. All the other great-grandfathers I know have full heads of hair, whatever color they want. Not mine.)

I looked away from him. Suddenly I realized what was wrong with his room. "Where's your flag?" I asked.

"I took it down."

I must have looked pretty funny. At least, the look on my face made him snort.

"How could you?" I asked in a whisper.

"It was easy," he said. "I just pulled out the tabs at the corners, and then—"

"Gran-Da!"

"Donald!" he replied. "When the government passed S.O.S., they took away the last thing that flag stood for. I don't want to look at it anymore."

He paused and stared at the floor for a while. I looked at the door, wondering if he would say anything if I just left.

Suddenly he looked up again. "Listen, Donald. I'm

ninety years old. That's not that old, these days—I could probably last another thirty."

That was no news. It was one of the reasons my mother was so upset when he moved in. I felt sorry for her. Thirty years of Gran-Da was my idea of a real nightmare.

"The thing is," he continued, "I'm just a normal guy, not a hero. But sometimes there's something you have to do, no matter what it costs you."

I looked at him in horror. "You're not going to do anything crazy, are you?" I felt sick in my stomach. Didn't he understand he could get us *all* in trouble? If he wasn't careful, the Uncles might come and take us away. I glanced at the ceiling, half expecting it to open up so that a giant hand could reach down and snatch my great-grandfather then and there.

"Why are you telling me this?" I asked at last.

"Maybe I'm hoping that if I scare you enough it will make you start to think." He shrugged. "Or maybe I just want to see what you'll do."

"Can I go now?"

"Yeah," he said bitterly. "Go on. Get out of here."

I slipped out of his room and ran down the hall to my own room. I flopped onto my bed and lay there, staring up at my beautiful flag and trembling.

I thought about Gran-Da all that night. I thought about him in school the next morning, while we were saying the pledge, and the Lord's Prayer, and reciting the names of the presidents. I remembered what Gran-Da had said the first time he heard me recite the list—that there had been more presidents than we were naming, that some of them were being left out.

I wanted to talk to my teacher, but I was afraid.

The next morning was Saturday. When Gran-Da came to breakfast he had a red band tied around his head. He was wearing a vest with fringe on it, a blue shirt, and faded blue pants; he was carrying a lumpy plastic bag. He had a button on his vest that looked like an upside-down Y with an extra stick coming out of it.

"What's that?" I asked, pointing to the button.

"A peace symbol," he said. He dropped the bag to the floor and settled into his chair.

"Really, Arthur," said my mother. "Don't you think this is carrying things a little too far?"

"S.O.S. was carrying things too far," said Gran-Da.

My father sighed. "Look, Grampa, it's not really a problem. If you don't break the rules, S.O.S. won't have any effect on you."

I was amazed to hear him say that. Then I decided he must be trying to get Gran-Da to calm down. It didn't work. Gran-Da shook his head stubbornly, and suddenly I knew what he had in the bag.

My throat got thick with fear. I couldn't finish my breakfast.

After breakfast I followed Gran-Da out of the house. He was heading for the town square. I was pretty sure I knew what he was planning. My stomach was churning. What if the Uncles thought he had polluted our whole family?

I could only think of one way to save us. I slipped into a televid booth to call my Uncle. When I told him what was happening he looked stern and shocked.

"You won't hold this against the rest of us, will you?" I asked nervously.

He shook his head. "Of course not," he said. "You've done the right thing. We'll have to come and talk to all of you when this is over, of course. But I wouldn't worry about it much."

The screen went blank. I hurried back out to the street.

I felt embarrassed, and frightened. But I was also a little excited. Would the S.O.S. men really show up? My friends would think I was a real hero. I hurried toward the town square.

Gran-Da was already there. He had climbed onto the bandstand, of all places, and he was shouting about S.O.S.

People looked at him nervously. To my surprise, a few actually stopped to listen. I stood beneath a large tree, about a hundred feet away. I didn't want to get too close.

Suddenly Gran-Da reached into the bag and pulled out the flag he had taken off his wall the night before. Holding the upper edge, he rolled it over the side of the bandstand. A slight breeze made the stripes slide and shift.

I covered my face with my hands and wished the terrible scene would end.

Where were the S.O.S. men?

"Friends!" cried Gran-Da. "When I was a boy, this piece of cloth used to stand for something. Yes, it did. In fact, it stood for a whole lot of things. Ideas. Like that a man should be free to say what he thinks, and worship where he wants, and get together with other folks if it pleases him."

More people were stopping to listen now. Someone started to boo.

"But that's all over," shouted Gran-Da. "Bit by bit, piece by piece, we've given away all the things this used to stand for. S.O.S. was the end of it. Now this poor old flag doesn't stand for anything at all.

"That being so, I think it's time I put it out of its misery."

I looked around. Where were the S.O.S. men? Why didn't they get here?

Now that people realized what Gran-Da was going to do, they started to back away. Some of them left. I could tell that others wanted to, wanted to get as far away from the terrible thing he was about to do as they possibly could. But they couldn't bring themselves to go. They wanted to see if he would really do it.

Gran-Da raised the flag and lit a match.

"Good-bye, Old Glory," he said sadly. "It was a good idea while it lasted."

He touched the corner of the flag with the match. Nothing happened, of course, since like all flags it was made of flameproof material. You can't burn a flag even if you try.

Gran-Da knew that. He wasn't stupid—just crazy. A crazy, dangerous person—the kind who could ruin the wonderful country we've built.

Suddenly I saw the S.O.S. men. They looked beautiful in their blue pants, white shirts, and red vests.

Gran-Da saw them too. I know he did.

So it's not like it's my fault, really. He had a chance. Everyone knows that even though the new law allows for instant executions, the Shoot On Sight men are supposed to give a guy a chance.

But Gran-Da didn't care. When his first match went out he lit another one. He held it to the corner of the fireproof flag and just stood there smiling at the three men.

So everyone could see that he was crazy.

The men lifted their laser rifles. The leader counted to three, and they fired in unison.

The light sliced right through the old man. He toppled over the edge of the bandstand. The flag curled around him as he fell. He was still holding it when he hit the ground.

My throat got thick. I could feel tears at the corners of my eyes. Crazy, I know. But he was my great-grandfather, after all. So I don't think it was too bad to feel a *little* sad about what had happened.

That doesn't mean I don't think I did the right thing by calling the S.O.S. guys. I mean, think about it. What would happen if other people started to think like Gran-Da—crazy things, like that everybody should be allowed to say whatever they wanted to?

What kind of a world would that be?

ABOUT THE AUTHORS

BRUCE COVILLE is a well-known children's book writer whose work ranges from picture books, such as *Sarah's Unicorn*, to young adult novels, such as *My Teacher Is an Alien*. He has edited several anthologies, including *The Unicorn Treasury* and *Herds of Thunder, Manes of Gold*. He also writes musical plays that have been produced around the country. He lives in New York City.

KARA DALKEY is, by day, a word processor for an insurance brokerage. At night and on weekends, she is a novelist and a short story writer. A resident of Minneapolis, she is also a musician (electric bass), artist, radio dramatist, sky diver, and karate student. She is currently working on her fifth adult fantasy novel set in sixteenth-century India. Her other novels include *The Curse of Sagamore*, *The Nightingale*, *The Word of Sagamore*, and *Euryale*.

CAROL FARLEY considers herself among the world's most enthusiastic science fiction fans. Her first sf story, "The DILOPS Are Coming," was published in

Anywhere, Anywhen. She has had seven mystery novels published and other nonmystery novels, including the Golden Kite Award–winning *The Garden Is Doing Fine*. She lives in Roscommon, Michigan.

JOE HALDEMAN is one of the most respected science fiction writers in America. Poet, short story writer, novelist, he has won the Hugo and Nebula awards for his fiction and the Rhysling for his sf poetry. His best-known book is *The Forever War*, but he has written many more. He lives both in Boston—where he teaches at MIT—and in Florida—where he and his wife, Gay, make their permanent home.

PEG KERR was born and raised in a suburb of Chicago and now lives in Minneapolis. Her first paycheck from her first job went to pay for a science fiction writing course where she met her husband and wrote this story. Her fiction has appeared in *Amazing Stories*, *Pulphouse*, and *Tales of the Unanticipated*.

ANNE MCCAFFREY's Pern novels, starring the wonderful dragons, have remained sf best-sellers for years. One of science fiction's most popular authors, she raises horses on her farm Dragonhold in Ireland.

PATRICIA A. MCKILLIP's RiddleMaster of Hed trilogy established her as one of the finest fantasy writers for young adults. She has a number of novels out for both children and adults. Some are fantasy, some are science fiction, and some are simply realistic. She lives in Roxbury, New York.

RESA NELSON, a 1985 graduate of Clarion, the preeminent sf writer's conference, has had several short stories published. She lives in Massachusetts and is working on her first novel.

SUSAN SHWARTZ is a financial writer and editor for a Wall Street investment firm. Her other full-time job is that of a science fiction and fantasy writer. She has published over thirty stories, five anthologies, and seven novels, including a collaboration with Andre Norton entitled *Imperial Lady*. She holds a Ph.D. in English literature from Harvard and lives in Forest Hills, New York.

DAVID ALEXANDER SMITH is the author of three sf novels for adults—*Marathon*, *Rendezvous*, and *Homecoming*. A past treasurer of the Science Fiction Writers of America, he lives in Cambridge, Massachusetts.

NANCY SPRINGER's ten novels of mythic fantasy include the Sea King trilogy and *Chains of Gold*. She has also written a number of books for young readers about horses—including *Not on a White Horse* and *They're All Named Wildfire*. The mother of two, she lives with her husband and children, a guitar, and a Sheltie in Dallastown, Pennsylvania.

CONNIE WILLIS has won three Nebula and two Hugo awards for her short fiction. Before becoming a science fiction writer, she was a fifth-grade teacher and still frequently teaches writing in the public schools. She lives in Greeley, Colorado.

JANE YOLEN is the author of well over one hundred books and has been called "America's Hans Christian Andersen." Her popular science fiction books include *Dragon's Blood*, *Heart's Blood*, and *A Sending of Dragons*, collectively known as the Pit Dragon Trilogy, and a time travel novel called *The Devil's Arithmetic*. Her book *Owl Moon*, illustrated by John Schoenherr, won the 1988 Caldecott Medal. She is a past president of the Science Fiction Writers of America and lives in Hatfield, Massachusetts.